# A Fate Better Than Life

Marcus Dailly

# DEDICATION

For Cliona, Cillian and Ellen and my late dad Dan, gone but never
forgotten.

# CONTENTS

# 1
## June 2013- A Home From Home

The inevitability that life's time cycle rolls perpetually to its natural, grim conclusion is enough to blacken even the most optimistic soul. Not, however, in the curious world according to Alexander Pace. In fact, Alexander Pace positively luxuriates in the ravages his body clock inexorably sets upon him. He does not fear the dwindling of time, the unrelenting vertiginous decline of mind, body and spirit, but embraces it like he would a new born child; another chance at a life he thought had passed him by.

Revelling smugly in the fraying book ends of his life, Alexander Pace is holed up where the air is musty, the sun stained curtains tainted beige and the roles of adults and children are blurred into seemingly terminal reversal. While most of his advancing years peer bleakly through their fingers at their diminishing bodies and impending demise, Alexander Pace relishes it like a toddler does Christmas.

One nudged single run past 70 years, this glorious final innings, Alexander Pace believes, will be his finest- his maiden chance to secure the contentment that has eluded him during a troubled knock. Now, here he prematurely abides, the self-believing Lord of an undesirable Manor where cheery faced nurses pander to his whimsical demands and his daily routine revolves around others' mortalities.

Gazing wondrously out the bay window of The Riverview Nursing and Retirement Home, he overlooks Dundee's burgeoning waterfront area. To Alexander Pace it is an idyllic sight; the early morning sun shimmering laconically on the still silver waters of the moody River Tay, the peaceful scene punctuated only by the cawing of a storm crow and the faint sigh of a commuter train wheezing intently over the imposing steel girders of the rail bridge as it sweeps majestically across to the tumbling, lazy shores of Fife. With a long, soft and wrinkled hand he smudges the dew from the whitening window, his elongated skeletal fingers smearing the moisture onto his paisley patterned house coat. Momentarily, a morbid cloud threatens to balaclava the sun like a lump of steel wool painting a looming shadow over a curious room. The room that the cloud temporarily cloaks is home to 'those eccentric brothers', a moniker that they have unwittingly adopted. Alexander Pace calls this room home. His twin brother certainly does not.

For Alexander Pace, though, nothing else matters but the next second that ticks away from him, the next wave that laps calmly ashore. Every second brings him closer to the redemption he believes another life can give, a second further away from the gnawing heartache his previous life has dictated.

This now is the life he has craved; a life of ever dwindling responsibilities, a life where others tend to his every whim, a life where the key to his calamitous past remains firmly padlocked in a closet with no decipherable code.

Alexander Pace glances at a rickety watch that sits ill fittingly on his waspish wrist. Somehow he is undaunted by each second that bounds eagerly away, he desperately wants to freeze the past into the annals of time and thaw into a future that he believes can offer an improved fate.

A fate better than life.

# 2
# PEBBLED SHORE

Alexander Pace surveys the twin room in which he now blissfully resides. Twin being the operative word. Though his body remains a relatively well-oiled machine and his mental faculties are in nearly perfect working order, Alexander Pace loves to be old before his time. Old age is what he desperately desires and this muggy nursing home is where he hopes his sands of time will drip drearily dry.

Creaking opening the sun bleached curtains, a single cone of dusty light sets a harvest yellow haze over the tattered, ageing furniture and the depressing pea green wall paper that imprisons the room. On top of the moody fawn dressing table lies a copy of a poem. It is set, pride of place, on smoky yellow paper and framed in a tarnished faux silver frame. Unlike its one careful owner, the years have taken their toll on the script's appearance, but, for Alexander Pace, time holds firm with its sentiments. The poem scribed on the tainted amber paper is William Shakespeare's Sonnet Number 60. It is Alexander Pace's favourite work of poetic literature and one which he believes echoes the meanders of his life.

Whilst other children in his Primary School class were reading nursery rhymes about the fetching of water pails or Aesop fabling about boys crying wolf, Alexander's mother was helping him to unpick and analyse the intricacies of the Bard's Sonnets. It was his soothing bed time read. Before the turn of his first decade, he had settled on Shakespeare's Sonnet Number 60 as his favourite, painting a pictorial prelude to the life he now leads:

*'Let the waves make towards the pebbled shore,*

*So do our minutes hasten to their end,*

*Each changing place with that which goes before*

*In sequent toil all forwards do contend.'*

Alexander still habitually consumes the words of the Sonnet each day, if for no other reason but to make his late mother proud. Now, like the waves that Shakespeare described as ebbing and flowing incessantly and destructively towards the pebbled shore, he celebrates how the minutes of his life are unceasingly tickling away from him. He rejoices in the ravages that these redoubling waves take on his body as he toils and crawls beyond maturity towards a different life. A life he hopes is removed from his difficult past.

Alexander Pace's coveted and closeted upbringing hints at a man whose life would take an unconventional route. In truth his life has meandered on a curious journey, a gruelling hike propelled by hidden grief and gut wrenching inner turmoil. It has been a life where Alexander has been unable to fully cement his place, make his stamp, forge a future. Every time he ever thought he was arriving somewhere, placing his feet firmly on the rocky road to contentment, the rug was hauled unceremoniously from under him, most hurtfully by some of those who supposedly loved him.

The mere inkling that his thoughts might turn turning towards those dark times provoke an involuntary twitch in Alexander, an unconscious shake of the head like a flee ridden dog wafting free its intolerable nemesis.

So, who exactly is the real Alexander Pace? Does anyone even know? Does he even know? Even his name has undergone several forms of reconstruction. He has been Alexander to some, Alex to others, he was Ecky to the mockers and Eck to most who knew him best. Not since, as an infant, his doting mother insisted he was referred to by his Sunday name has he been Alexander. Chameleonic name, chameleonic nature- a life spent struggling to find his niche in an existence fashioned largely by old fashioned heartbreak. Now, again, like the long lost mother he spends few seconds not thinking about would say, 'the name is Alexander, please don't do me the disservice of shortening its importance.'

Now the nurses in The Riverview Nursing and Retirement Home, call him as he demands. He adores the feeling that they dance to his every tune- the sound of his proper name is symphonic to his unrequired hearing aid. Alexander loves how the female nurses dote on him- it gives him a sense of importance in an almost utopic setting where he is indulged and bathes in the soapy bubbles of imagined superiority and respect he has long craved. 'Would you like more carrot soup Alexander? Would you like me to fetch you today's newspaper Alexander? How many sugars would you like in your Earl Gray tea Alexander? Now, here, please let me puff up that plump cushion under your back Alexander. Alexander, would you like a little jam with your scone?' Blissful words indeed. The fawning, the indulgence, the slavish attention at the drop of a handkerchief and, most of all, the female touch, the female touch he has spent years and years craving – now he has discovered his perfect pre cursor to what he hopes is an impending heavenly demise.

# 3
## NOTHIN' BUT AN ECKY PACE

Alexander reaches for the small of his back and inhales sharply, his upper lip curling above his (own) teeth and his sharp eyes grimace deliberately to illustrate his pain:

' My bloody back's at me again I'll tell you George. Every day there's something different. I'll tell you, at my age, it is not half catching up with me, all these ailments I'm afflicted by every day. What with the brittle bones and then there's the migraines and the insomnia, and don't forget about the attacks of anxiety. I mean George, how many things can one man rightly have wrong with him at one time? If it is not a physical ailment, it is a mental one. I really must see Doctor Dawson about those this week. I'll have a bloomin' season ticket with that Doctor soon! Deary, deary me. George... Eh, George are you paying any notice of me? George. George!' he says raising the volume to just below a shout.

' I'm in pain, would you please pass me that liniment over would you,' he groans exaggeratedly, deliberately gaining the attention of a quarrelsome looking individual who wears a brooding scowl at the other side of the room.

This man is George, George Pace. George Pace bristles; his robust, muscular forearms leaning aggressively on the arms of an ageing wine leather sitting chair positioned in the corner of the room. George Pace is Alexander's brother, twin brother, non-identical. To say non-identical implies a passing resemblance, a similarity of look and personality derived from a shared embryo. But not only are Alexander and George non-identical, they are non-alike-in-anyway-shape-or-form-whatsoever. They are, in every way but nature, bi-polar entities. The phrase chalk and cheese was coined for these siblings, they make Danny and Arnie look like doppelgangers.

George is gruff, gritty and combustible; a dry keg of powder with its blue touch paper waiting to ignite. His lugubrious demeanor is so

6

unchangingly mirthless that it cannot be irrelevant; his ever downcast eyes, his heavy tread, his pendulous top lip that could thwart a smile if Alexander got his bow tie caught in a mangle. Alexander, in contrast, is a more acquired taste; languid and laconic and decidedly unaggressive with a putty soft centre , palatable to most, but gets up the noses of others. Just ask his twin brother.

Their physical appearances tell some truths about their personalities, but belie what is going on beneath the façade. George's short, squat frame is held firm by bow legs and crowned by a balding head that is home only to sporadic grey hairs. Alexander is finer looking, many would say he's handsome for his age with a refined look that carries unblemished skin. His frame is thin and lanky creating an illusionary tale as he appears to dwarf his brother by even more than the seven inches that the measuring tape suggests.

But lurking ominously beneath the unblemished surface creeps a troubled and tarnished mind, his fresh face a mask that cloaks the gut-wrenching loss and betrayal that has left him hiding a fractured heart that has never truly healed and, without George, would have been fatally broken. Alexander has inserted a buffer in his mind, a selectively permeable membrane that siphons the corrosive thoughts of past experiences that came inches from destroying him. Instead he channels his focus on what he hopes will be a rose tinted procession towards an ultimate meeting with his maker.


' Jesus wept Eck, yisterdy it was yir knee, the day it's yir back, the morn it'll likely be yir heart. At this rate yi'll be deed by the morn's afternoon. That's if luck has anything ti do we it. Anyway, it's no a season ticket you need wi that poor doctor it's a bleedin' day pass- an every day pass. Now leave me in peace to read the day's paper,' George barks back with an acidic lashing of the tongue, his coarse Dundee brogue perfected from years of working relentlessly on the city's factory floors. In every way George represents the absolute antithesis of his brother's refinery.

A stoic man by nature, nurture has made him a working class grafter and now he yearns longingly for the return of the days when he worked his knuckles to the bone in the city's factories; he loved the graft, the camaraderie, the kinship, the togetherness, the drinks with his mates on a Friday afternoon in the heaving Trades House Bar where all the workers would gather and share stories of their week over cold pints of golden lager. But more than anything, he misses being with the love of his life, the kindred spirit who he supposed he would share all his days with. But fate, and his brother, intervened and conspired against the ambitions of his heart. It is better to have loved and lost than never to have loved at all is what they say. Try telling that to George Pace and have him believe you. George has been the loser by choice and that makes it all the tougher.

For George, the days of his past life are so infinitely removed from his current existence, because that's what it is to him, it is an existence it is certainly not a life. George never asked to be cooped up in The Riverview Nursing and Retirement Home and nor does he need to be. George is not ready for the knacker's yard yet- other than the walking stick to aid his arthritic knees, he is as fit as a butcher's pencil and thumb tack sharp in mind. Every day when he looks at the ageing reflection that scowls crossly back at himself in the mirror of the tiny room he endures, he reminds himself that he is doing this for his twin brother, just as he promised his late mother he would.

Unlike his brother he doesn't view a day trip in the minibus to the local garden centre for afternoon tea, coffee and jam scones with the care home squad as his idea of a fulfilling day out. A trip to Starbucks that Alexander treats like a trip to heaven's gates is George's perfect idea of a bloody Hell. For George Pace this is a fate far worse than death.

He knows that, without Alexander, he could have been someone of his own making, led the life he wished for; achieved ambitions, maintained love, reared a family. Instead here he is, driven by fierce loyalty, sitting in an old folks' home waiting for his next serving of gruel in the land of the bewildered and the bewildering. He shakes his head like a dog flicking water from its nose:

'One day's peace that's all eh ask Eck, just one day's peace fae you. There's bugger all wrang wee yir bloody back and if your bones are brittle then I'm Pope Gregory the Ninth. Remember, you're the reason em in this godforsaken hole in the first place so the least you could do is keep yir puss shut for fev minutes 'til eh read the day's sport's news because sure as fate you'll be grabbing this paper to read aboot yir beloved flaming funerals the first chance that yi get,' he roars shaking his rolled up copy of the Dundee Courier and Advertiser in his venous right hand.

Funerals are George's biggest bug bear and represent everything about the life that he has been cajoled into that he abhors. Alexander has transformed himself into the funeral fraternity's answer to a wedding crasher, gatecrashing the ceremonies of unsuspecting families during their moments of heart rending loss. Every morning, whether bathed in sunshine or dampened by rainfall, Alexander starts his day the same way, by scouring the hatch, match and dispatch section of his local paper, glossing over the irrelevances of the joyous newborns and happy couples. Why celebrate procreation and nuptials when there are people's lives to be remembered and celebrated? That is the mantra that he now lives by. Recently he has even taken his habit into the 21st century, using the communal computer in the residential area to sign up for a macabre website called www. r.i.p.co.uk which ghoulishly e mails its subscribers all the breaking funeral news and allows him to scribe heartfelt messages of condolence to the families of dead people they know or, in Alexander's case, people he claims to have met, but usually hasn't.

To subscribe he had to list details like age, city he lived, common interests to focus the e-mails he received to people similar to himself, but he lied blatantly to ensure that he widened the net. Alexander sees these depressing ceremonies as a means of socialising, a gathering of people he either barely knows or doesn't know at all but can sympathise with, be their equal for the day, a shoulder to cry on, even a friend.

The past week alone has seen the brothers attend three funeral services- Angela Flannery, a 69 year old woman who had worked as a cashier in the Royal Bank of Scotland branch on Strathmartine Road and who may have served Alexander a few times. John Wilson, a 79 year old electrician who Alexander thought had once replaced the faulty tube in his TV set and Paul Byrne who, as far as George is aware, was an 80 year old time served plumber who Alexander had never even met, though he claims that he changed the element in his boiler around 40 years ago.

Every day, Alexander seeks out a link to his past, a link to someone he knows. Any link will do, the more tenuous the better to enable him to slip discreetly and quietly into the funeral and nonchalantly mingle with anonymity among the mourners, desperately hoping to increase his circle of acquaintances through the grief of others. He believes that he can play the part of the sympathetic, popular man about town; a role in life he craved but could never achieve, but through others' fatalities he believes he just might get there after all.

Habitually, Alexander refrains from reaction. He never does. His 71 years have told him that George doesn't really mean these blustering diatribes, 'He's just letting off steam', their mother used to say, 'give him a minute and he'll be fine. It will soon pass by.' Crouching over and clawing at the alleged pain in his back, Alexander liberally applies more liniment oil to the small of it, catching a peek of George out of the corner of his eye as he does so. Demonstrably George thwacks the paper open with an exaggerated jut, nearly ripping it at the spine.

' Bloody malingerer,' he mutters a grunt under his breath, ' One of these bloody days em gonna walk oot o this godforsaken hell hole of a place for good and see how yi'd get on then. To think what eh could have had if it wisnae for you. Now eh spend meh whole life tryin' tae find fuckin' funerals tae go to, ' he fumes, a reddening hue enveloping his furrowed, well-worn brow.

' Watch not to rip that paper George, we need it to plan our day's events. We would get nothing planned without our daily edition of the Courier now would we?' Alexander replies patronisingly as he nonchalantly checks for dirt beneath his trimmed finger nails, blissfully ignoring his bullish brother's jibes. Alexander is relaxed in the confidence that his George's aggressively delivered words, though hurtful, are sieve like in their ability to hold water with him. Carefree, he tightly screws the sticky top of the liniment bottle and places it on his bedside cabinet, and nestles it neatly between a plethora of products and potions he uses to soothe the limbs he wants everyone to believe are creaking to breaking point. Stretching his back with the soft palms of his hands, he lets out an audible groan, feeling George's scowling eyes burning a crater in his neck. Alexander knows his twin brother well enough to predict that his frustrated sigh is his first sign of relenting. Alexander stifles a smirk, it's a battle he is well used to winning.

' Right, give me that pen here right the noo. And yi ken what, I'll tell you this for bugger all, this is the last day em dayin this, the very last. Em no spendin any mare o meh life lookin fir funerals for you. Do you hear me Eck? That's the fuckin truth.'

' I do and it's Alexander, not Eck.' he replies snootily faking the faux posh accent that he has acquired, ' And George, please stop using the f word would you? It's not at all becoming.'

' Eck, why don't you just fuck off?'

# 4
# KILLJOY

Alexander casts an approving, rheumy eyed gaze around the brothers' room. To those who prefer their tumblers half full it is minimalist and understated, the half empty brigade would deem it bare, miserable and utterly depressing. The brothers naturally disagree on the merits of their current living quarters. To Alexander this is his idea of heaven, for George it's a living quarter just a grid mark shy of Hell's gates.

The sun stares confidently into the brothers' room, bathing George's mahogany bedside cabinet in glorious sunshine where a solitary yellow lampshade broods and is held up by the porcelain frame of a naked, statuesque Victorian female. Other than that it is bare, lonely, but unruffled. Alexander's cabinet is the binary opposite. Draped in the shadows of the curtains, it is a cluttered piece of furniture on which three photograph frames lurk partially in view behind his raft of toiletries, potions and medicines and his beloved copy of Shakespeare's Sonnet 60. The small pale blue frame on the right contains a picture of the twin brothers on their first day at secondary school, a large cream frame in the middle with a picture of their parents in happy matrimony and a faceless black frame which sits somewhat skewed in blank and dormant solitude.

'It's a most beautiful day out there today George, I feel so privileged to be alive and living in such a beautiful setting. Don't you? I hope I have a few years left, but with my health lately I am not so sure. What with the brittle bones and the kidney stones and the back and the eyes and I can feel another bloody chest infection marching mercilessly towards me shouting 'I'm gonna finish this cripple off once and for all," muses Alexander, in a futile attempt to encourage his brother's concentration.

For George the beautiful weather represents a pathetic fallacy. He ignores the details of the sick note, it has become a white fuzzy background noise to him now, but retorts with a snappy vehemence, 'Eh, the perfect day tae watch other folks' bloody misery is what you really mean. Like there's bugger all else we could be dayin' on a day like this, but going to a bloody funeral.'

' Oh stop being such a blooming killjoy and read the names from the paper would you,' Alexander replies dismissively rubbing his right eye.

' My eyes are at me again you know, it must have been that cream I put on them last night before bed to keep them soothed. And here's me just over the blooming cold that struck me down last week, not to mention the fact that I can feel those kidney stones might be about to make an unwanted appearance. Again. They say kidney stones are worse than child birth you know- and I'm sure women would argue with that- but when you have brittle bones and a bad back like mine too then it makes things a hundred times worse. Now, please, if you may… ' he says rubbing his eyes again in an effort to garner the sympathy he constantly craves, '…could you read the names please George?'

George glares incredulously at his brother, but sits on his thoughts. Any riposte would only increase his fury and provide the reaction his brother seeking. 'This is the last time em dain this, I'm tellin yi that for nothin', he mutters internally unsure if he has communicated his feelings out aloud, not that it would alter the odds if he had.

' Alphabetically as you normally do my good brother, my eyes are at me today or I'd read it myself. I'd be quicker at any rate.' It's the type of sly dig that Alexander indulges in and George ignores. Alexander loves the feeling that he is his brother's intellectual superior and has no qualms in reminding him so on a daily basis.

' If I hear about those eyes one mare time em gonna….'

' George, the names. Now please,' Alexander demands.

' Eh'll just read the names o' the folk yid maybe ken, just tae save time,' says George warming ever so slightly to the task.

' How would you know who I'd know George? You might be my twin brother, but you are not actually me are you? Now stop being so silly and read them all please George,' snipes Alexander patronisingly.

'Because Eck, eh've been stuck we you fir 71 years and, in ah that you've hardly any mates and anyone yi do ken is either deid or yi ken them through me. That's how eh ken wha you ken?'

Alexander pleads ignorance to his twin's snappy riposte, 'Nonsense, now just read the list please George and do it smartly.'

'Gie me a second, em trying tae find the tap o the list,' grunts George faintly, his enthusiasm for the battle starting to dwindle.

Physically, the battle of the brothers would be a catch weight contest. If it came to blows it would be like Cassius Clay with a machete fighting a Swiss Army Knife wielding disabled dwarf, but in many ways George, despite retaining much of the tautness of his youth, feels intimidated by his brother's way with words, his ability to communicate making him feel somewhat inferior. This has been true since childhood despite Alexander's gangly, often waspish, appearance. As a child he grew and grew so much that he gave the appearance of a veal calf who had been stretched in a crate, all pale and scared of himself like a shaved horse.

Stereotypes would suggest that George was the brawn, Alexander the brains. They had been pigeon holed from a young age; Alexander the academic, George the factory fodder, his father's son who followed in the footsteps of generations of Paces who served their time grafting on factory production lines. George senior's rough edges surrounded stoic working class values and ethics. ' Yi dinnae need pieces o paper we qualifications on them to make an honest living like your father George. Tak it fae me, this is a real man's job a proper way to earn your crust,' he was regularly told.

George idolised his father, he was the personification of the autocratic spirited man he wanted to grow up to be. George Senior had also been involved in amateur running with the Dundee Hawkhill Harriers, a passion that he encouraged George to share. When he turned his hand to coaching, he had a reputation in the town of training his athletes like whippets and tried to keep them away from the lady whippets in fear that they would tease and tempt them away from the track. George was brought up on a diet of egg whites and milk which his father believed would enhance his sprinter's speed and in during his early secondary school days his diet worked. George was a very good sprinter, as a 13 year old he was fourth in the Scottish Schools, running 11 and a half seconds on a wet track, his record was 11 seconds dead on dry grass. At that time, everyone wanted to win the hundred yards and George's father believed with more training and a stricter egg white and milk routine, his son could win gold for Scotland at the Commonwealth Games, an ambition he would dearly loved him to see through.

But much as he loved the running it didn't satisfy the amount of aggression inside him and football was his real first love. Unfortunately his aggressive style of play put paid to any chance of George carving a career as a footballer or an athlete and his dad spent more time in Dundee Royal Infirmary waiting for his son's broken shoulder blade, ankles and kneecaps to be plastered up than he did watching him at the side of the pitch.

' Eh told you that you should've stuck with the runnin' son, yi would nae be a physical wreck by the time your 16 if you had only listened to your old man,' his father would preach to him.

It is advice that George wishes every day that he could reverse the clock and tune in to. His father's death hit George like a cannon ball. As a naïve 17 year old boy he was deprived of a father figure, but his dad's gritty spirit, often caustic tongue and deep seated family loyalty was passed down to him and was often masked by his brash outward demeanor.

Conversely, Alexander was your archetypical mummy's boy. The parents set the brother off on different tracks, journeys which would effectively form their personalities and lives. From birth Cathy preened and pandered to her youngest son (by 6 minutes and 43 seconds according to the birth certificates) and, through a combination of nature and nurture, they were cut out of the same cloth. She saw much of herself in Alexander. A qualified primary school teacher, she quit the profession she loved to look after and nurture the twins, reluctantly allowing George senior to win as much bread as his factory work would allow, when she knew she could've been bringing more to the table herself. The boys' parents were both only children meaning the family was bereft of an extended family network- no aunts, no uncles, no cousins and grandparents long having succumbed to the grim reaper's callings.

Their parents' individual roles within the family set up and what they brought to the household table were defined by the era they lived in. Acutely aware that the family never had the money to fund both brothers' academic aspirations Cathy made Alexander her project, she desperately wanted him to tread the road to academia that society had forced her to abandon, ' If you don't stick in you'll end up like your father, putting parts of machines together all day every day, day after day after day after day,' she would sneakily whisper to him out of the earshot of the madding duo.

She loved both brothers dearly, even though she would regularly complain to George that he was too often 'as crabbit as old Nick.' George never did find out who 'Old Nick' was, but he always assumed him to be someone of questionable temperament. His mum did, however, reserve the softest spot for young Alexander. This soft spot led the lads down separate paths, but their shared loins helped the glue stick closely enough that they were never parted despite their obvious differences. Whilst Alexander would sit at the kitchen table receiving help with his homework from his mother, George would be helping his father hammer up a bookshelf in the twins' bedroom or out in the street doing sprint sessions between the lamp posts or playing keepy ups with a brown, tattered leather ball. Cathy's cajoling and encouraging of Alexander proved successful and his grades at school won him the dux awards in English, Maths and French and fulfilled his mother's ambition of sending her boy to law school.

Cathy's death hit Alexander like an anvil. The swift nature of her demise through cancer only augmented his travails. For Alexander, at the age of just 38, it was the second blow in rapid succession that he has never truly recovered from. On her death bed she confided in George, whispering words cloaked in sorrowful regret, ' I am so sorry if you felt I wasn't a great mother to you George, but I truly love you both equally. Can you just promise me one thing? I think he is going to struggle to come to terms with my passing so soon after what happened to him last year. I know you are stronger and will cope just fine, but Alexander's heart is broken and this might crush him forever. Will you promise you will look after him for me? Would you do that for your mum please George?'

He camouflaged his emotions with a steely look as his stomach ached and heart churned inside, ' Nae bather mum.' His word is his honour where his brother is concerned.

# 5
## DISPATCHES

' Concentrate George! The list, would you read it,' urges Alexander, reviving George back into the present.

'Ok for fuck's sake would yi just give us a chance? Yir so flammin impatient when it comes to these bloody funerals. Now tune yir big lugs in and listen. Top o' the list the day is Baxter, Frank Iain Anthony- June 11<sup>th</sup> peacefully at his home after a long and courageous battle with illness. Frank Baxter, beloved husband and best...... '

' No A's today?' Alexander interrupts doubtingly.

'No, nae A's,' George replies definitely.

' Are you quite sure? That's very unusual is it not?'

' Do you no believe me or somethin? Nae A's died yisterday, what is so unusual aboot that? Do you want tae read yirsel?'

' No my eyes hurt.'

'So does meh heid. Frank Baxter beloved husband and best friend of Mora for 57 years.'

' Ah, now George, I do think I know him, is that not Robert Baxter's brother? You know Robert, the guy who used to run that coffee shop in the town across from the city churches? You know the one sits beside the steeple on the High Street? They make a lovely cappuccino in there and muffin for less than a fiver. You probably know him as Rab. It's his brother, I'm sure of it. Positive in fact. That's just a terrible shame. Eh, what time and where is it on? We'd better get ready. Oh God, I can't believe he's gone.'

' It isn't him and you dinna ken him. Rab died aboot ten year ago. Eh wiz at the funeral but you were not because yi didnae ken him. That was before you started going to funerals for fun and draggin muggings here alang we yi,' George says as his eyes remain fixed on the newspaper.

' No, sorry it's Mary Baxter's brother. You know Mary, she's involved with the Boys' Brigade? She used to run all the Church of Scotland fund raising coffee mornings. She would make the most delicious caramel shortcake, remember. Yes, sorry, that's who it is. How could I forget that? Gosh, Robert will miss that shortcake. I wonder if she'll make it for the wake? I'd love wee taste of that with a cup of tea.'

'Eck, It's a catholic ceremony and, if you listen, he doesnae even hae any brothers or sisters. It just speaks of him being the beloved husband of the late Norma and father of Jessica, Jonathon, Ian and Mellissa. So yi dinnae ken him, aright?'

' Damn, I thought we were in there George. All those bloody Baxters passing away and I don't even know any of them. It's bloomin' typical. I wonder if Robert's brother's still alive? I might search for him on rip.co.uk. Ok, anyway, never mind, they'll pass away sometime. Now, next one please, and can you read a little quicker? We don't have all day you know? ' Alexander said tapping his watch three times with the long index finger on his right hand.

George narrows his eyes and glares at him, ' Bent, Christopher, suddenly,' he says forcibly.

' Is that the Chris Bent from St Mary's, remember he used to drink in the Nine Maidens? He was a mechanic on Strathmartine Road, I'm sure of it. Oh, he was a lovely fellow so he was. He put oil in my engine for free one time when the red light came on. We'll have to go to that one, what time does it start? I'll get our trousers pressed...'

' You dinnae ken him either, he was only 21.'

' That's so, so tragic. Pass me my handkerchief will you George......?'

' He might be Christopher Junior though, the mechanic's son. Maybe we should go just in case.'

' His dad's is Eric, it says it right here in black and white.'

' Ah, that's a pity. Keep reading....'

' Sheila Bisset, Dessie Bradbury, Jason Bradbury, Alan Brett…,' continued Alexander apace, 'you dinnae ken any of them.'

' Slow down for goodness, sake. George would you just hold your horses for a minute. What was the name of the last one Alan Brett, I think I know his sister, she was…'

' You dinnae ken him. Now, moving on… Derek Brinning died peacefully in Ninewells Hospital after a long and brave battle with illness. Reposed at his home before mass on Saturday at….'

' Don't know him , move on. Read quicker George, read quicker, we don't have all day. This is not looking good today. What on earth are we going to do if there is no funeral to go to? There surely must be somebody on that bloomin' list, it's nearly the length of your arm.'

' We're only on bloody 'B' yi ken Eck,' George says with incredulity.

' Many more knock backs and I'll need to get Nurse Mabel to help me check my e-mails, you never know, I might've received some tip offs from my contacts on rip.co.uk.'

' What the hell are you whittering on aboot Eck? What the hell is an e-mail again? Is that they drugs the bairns take in the Mardi Gras night club? R.i.p Uk dot Co dot what? What the…..?' says George, totally perplexed by his brother's jargon.

' Oh, nothing, now read on George. You need to get into the 21$^{st}$ century, you're 71 not 171 you know. Anyway, keep going, we will need to go to one today with any luck. I'm confident about these B's….' Alexander shuffles in his seat.

'Brown, James, June 10$^{th}$, aged 82, peacefully after a short illness in the care of the staff at Ninewells Hospital.'

Alexander's ears flare up like a phoenix from the flames, his eyes squinting in sudden deep concentration as he senses a genuine hit, ' Now that's our more like our demographic George my boy. Read on, read on quickly please,' he urges, shuffling his canoe like feet closer to his brother with all the anticipation of an eager schoolboy at a 6$^{th}$ year disco.

' Demo? Demo what? What the devil are you talking aboot Eck?'

' Nothing, now quickly read on, we've no time to waste with,' Alexander tuts incongruously, frantically waving his hand to hurry the reading along.

'Brown, James, June 10th, aged 82, peacefully after a short illness in the care of the staff at Ninewells Hospital. Sadly missed by his loving wife Jane and his dotting children Alison and Jack. He will be remembered with love by all his family and friends. Funeral service this evening 5 o'clock in Downfield Church. Burial afterwards at the Downfield Hotel, all very welcome. Family flowers only please. Donations to the Society for the Hard of Hearing would be greatly appreciated,' George reads.

' That's James Brown, that's Jimmy Brown! You remember him George,' he squawks, nearly jumping from his chair.

' Who the hell's Jimmy Broon? I've never heard o anyone called Jimmy Broon.'

' Do not give me that nonsense George. You know Jimmy and it's Brown not Broon. Remember I used to play football with him with the Downfield? It must be him, the service is at Downfield church.'

' Eck, remember, you never played fitba. You were shite at it, remember? You played one game ever for the Doonfield and that was only cos we were short o players and eh asked yi tae play. You were worse than a man doon, the only player ever to be taken off when we had nae left subs to replace you with. You were walking aboot too afraid tae tackle anyone, claimin' tae be injured. After that game anyone who we thought was faking an injury was called an 'Ecky Pace.' That's how brave you were,' George says shaking his head, but Alexander is unrepentant.

' Oh give over George, I wasn't that bad and my name is Alexander remember. Anyway, enough of this nonsense, that funeral is our former football team mate Jimmy Brown. We have to go to that, it would not be right to miss it. It would be highly disrespectful in fact. What would his family think if we just chose not to show up, that would be a damned down disgrace?' Alexander says excitedly.

' What would his family think?' George roars. ' Eh'll tell you what they'd think. They'd think who the fuck are these two stupid lookin' buggers standing on their own at the back o the church. Eh played aboot five games o' fitba wi Jimmy Broon and that wis mare than 50 years ago. Eh've no seen the poor bugger since the day he left the Doonfield so there's nae chance yir getting' me tae his funeral. It might no even be the same Jimmy Broon,' George roars with an angry conviction.

' Don't you be so utterly ludicrous George. All his old team mates will be there. George it's a great chance to catch up with some of the boys. And of course it is the same Jimmy Brown, remember his girlfriend at that time was Alison Mayer, she was in your year at school. I think she was held back a year with you too. She must have married him. George, it is him. We must go. I am going without you if you don't,' Alexander proclaims.

As George refuses to bite, Alexander plays his well-worn petted lip routine, the doe eyed, hard done by look that he has perfected over the years when he doesn't get his way. More still, he knows George is a sucker for it. Despite his angry exterior, Alexander believes that he has him wrapped around his wrinkled finger, he always has. George has form for crumbling to his brother's demands. Why would he not crumble this time? Plus he owes him one doesn't he?

' Right, ok, but this is the flammin' last time eh dae this fir you. As long as yi ken that I'm sneaking in at the back and then sneaking oot five minutes before the end. Em no standing with his family askin' who the fuck I am,' George says relenting.

' Absolutely George, I agree. Now let's go for breakfast, Nurse Mabel will be furious if we are late again. I wonder what's on the menu today? I fancy some scrambled eggs I think,' Alexander says smugly trying to return the conversation to normality.

As George folds his paper down and places it open on the crossword page on the cabinet beside him, he thinks he hears Alexander try to hide a giggle.

# 6
# MABEL

The day's activities 'agreed', there is an almost inaudible chap at the door, followed without response by the sound of the metallic lock squeezing and the handle creaking at a turn. The door ambles ajar and then is pushed heavily opened with gusto. Standing at the threshold is a nurse; a cheerful looking woman around half the brothers' age. Her face has a sallow glow and is annotated by flushed purple cheeks, deep blue eyes and a white bandana that holds her jet black hair hostage from her forehead. George denies her presence even a cursory glance turning his paper to the simplex crossword, clicking the nib of his pen demonstrably to attention. Alexander, on the other hand, shuffles excitedly to attention and makes no effort to contain the delight that her appearance has brought him.

' Good morning Nurse Mabel. Is it not a beautiful day out there? I was just saying that to George a minute ago. It's so great to see you looking so well this morning,' Alexander says, sycophantically stretching out a slightly withered but wholly welcoming right hand.

Nurse Mable accepts his invitation with a faintly detectable nod and confidently enters the room accompanied by a soft whiff of lavender. Carrying herself impeccably in her perfectly pressed pale blue tunic and a navy cardigan which covers her ample shoulders, arms and back, she unconsciously observes the room's dusty imperfections which are highlighted by the summer sun's yellow harvest haze. ' Just as well the inspectors are not here today,' she almost thinks aloud. Nurse Mabel brings a breezy confidence with her into the room, a sweeping gust of efficiency.

' Good morning,' Nurse Mabel says, ' How are my two favourite brothers today? I trust you slept well again last night,' her words cheerfully bawling out of her rouged cheeks, her striking eyes flitting rapidly from one brother to the next whilst subconsciously noting the presence of George's flecked woollen trousers which are abandoned unceremoniously on the floor.

George grimaces, unsure if he really let that grunt out or held it hostage in his thoughts. George is suspicious by nature, often to a fault, and he finds Nurse Mabel's overt niceness as nauseating and difficult to swallow as the rice and raisin dessert they were served up as an accoutrement to last night's tea. George finds her fake, false, even contrived; it makes his skin crawl when she takes on that patronising, childish tone with him. George believes that he can see straight through the glare of her omnipresent sunny disposition.

Conversely, her motherly qualities captivate Alexander's interest. What George believes is an act, Alexander accepts as the genuine affection of a woman with his best interests at heart. Here is a pretty woman who is willing to indulge him, treat him well, respect his requests- everything he's ever desired in the female and everything he thought he once had access to forever but lost for good. Nurse Mabel radiates all the qualities that Alexander could ever have wanted in a woman and he bathes luxuriously in her indulgences. He doesn't take his eye off her as she briskly strides to the curtain, hauling them open with a firm hand. The sound of the metal hooks screeching to a halt across the rails provokes a forced tut from George- this time he hopes that Nurse Mabel notes his irritation.

Feeling the burn of her glare, he fills in 3 across – 'evil spirit'; starting with a 'g' and ending in a 't', 'should it not be starting with an 'M and ending in an l' he thinks to himself as he bores the word

GHOST aggressively into the crossword grid on his paper in black block capital letters.

' Oh yes Nurse Mabel, we slept quite delightfully, thank you so much for asking,' Alexander replies so sycophantically that George has to ignore the urge to add his own vomit to the fuzzy pea green carpet. ' Oh, just ignore George, I think he must have gotten out of the wrong side of the bed this morning,' he says nodding across the room, his eyebrows dancing to Nurse Mabel's tune.

' The bed's against the wall yi daft bastard, how could eh get oot the wrang side of it. Eh dinna want to be in the bloody uncomfortable bed o' nails in the first place. Eh hate this bleedin' place eh really do,' George snaps back, engaging fleeting eye contact with Nurse Mabel. Often he will say these things for a reaction, attempting to dangle the bait long enough for her to snap onto the hook.

But she offers him only a knowing smirk in riposte. Nurse Mabel likes to believe that she has George's number, 'Oh he just likes to play the grumpy old man, don't you George?' she teases so patronisingly that he half expects her to come over to him and tug at his cheeks. George elects to bite his tongue. He loathes the fact that she treats him like an impertinent school boy, he abhors being spoken to by this upstart as if he was still in his grey school shorts and long socks. Who does she think she is, the headmistress? Even as a child George found that type of condescending language irritating, but Alexander revels in her strict, but motherly manner. He loves to be spoken to like a child, he loves the reversal of the roles, it makes him feel worthwhile, indulged even.

' Now it's ten minutes to breakfast lads so is there anything you need help with before you come along? It's your favourite George, porridge with honey and bananas,' Nurse Mabel commands.

' She knows I hate bananas,' thinks George internally. ' And how dare she call me a lad, I've forgotten more than she's ever known.' 5

down – female dog starting with a 'b' and ending in a 'h', 'should it not be starting with an 'M and ending in an l' he thinks to himself as he bores the word BITCH into his paper in hard block capital letters without lifting his head an inch.

' Oh Nurse Mabel, my back is at me again, I wonder if you could do me the favour of rubbing a little of this oil onto it. I can't reach that far round because my shoulder's at me as well and I'm going to be on my feet a lot today so my brittle bones need some of your best attention,' he says in a tone that almost begs her to ask why.

' Oh, what do you have planned for the day?' she has taken the bait, fallen in hook line and sinker.

' It's terribly sad really, I feel tearful even saying it out loud. It's our old friend Jimmy Brown's funeral God rest his soul. We used to play football for Downfield with him back in the day. He is a sad loss. It is his wife Mary I'll feel most sorry for, she'll be heartbroken. She's been with him since they were at school you know, a classic childhood romance and it's survived the test of time,' he says pointing to the area on the small of his back where he wants Nurse Mabel to rub the liniment.

' Oh now, that's awfully sad,' she says, ' Now just you stand that way for me would you and I'll see to your back, we wouldn't want that causing you grief on another difficult day. It's been a tough time for you two, a lot of your friends seem to have been passing away. You seem to be at so many funerals, nearly two or three every week since you've been here,' she says sincerely, or sounding it at least, but George knows better, peering angrily over the rutted edges of his newspaper.

As Alexander groans in exhilaration, his brother considers letting his frustrations run away from him. He has to physically stop himself screaming out to Nurse Mabel that his brother's a fraud, that there's nothing wrong with his back, or his shoulder, or his knee, or his brittle bones or his ears or his heart or other parts of his body that are purportedly falling apart, allegedly crumbling in front of her and that they are only in here to satisfy his brother's craving to be loved and looked after- affections that have been too short in supply. He wants to blurt out that Alexander is a bloody Ecky Pace and that all these effing funerals that they go to are people that they barely fucking know and that his Eck, yes it's fucking Eck, only attends them to somehow appear the popular man about town that he had always craved to be, to show off the 'friends' that he imagined he'd have but never did in reality. He wants to scream and scream and scream 'til she stops rubbing his back with that stinking fucking liniment oil.

George knows that, if form is anything to go by, even after the inanities are complete, Nurse Mabel will be disinclined to leave. He had never sought to ask her a single question about herself because he could not care less for the answers. He does not want to know if she is married, or has kids or is happy in her job. The only thing he would like to say to her begins with the letter f, rhymes with cluck and ends in off.

But that would be cruel, it would be unjustified and, after all, Alexander is his brother and he likes Nurse Mabel's attention. But most of all, George knows more than anyone what Alexander has been through in his life, the heartache he has suffered. George promised on his mother's grave that he'd look after him. Blood is, after all, thicker than water, a point that George has to remind himself of regularly.

# 7
# LETTER

George stands as patiently as he can waiting while Alexander brushes his grey, shiny hair in the mirror and flosses his teeth which are all still his own despite his advanced years. ' I've spent half meh life waitin' on this bastard,' he thinks to himself, jabbing the ground with his crooked brown walking stick in frustration.

Time has taken its toll on George's joints and taut frame. While Alexander vocally claims the pain, George silently feels it. Riddled with rheumatism and arthritic pain in his limbs, he needs his stick to carry his creaking knee joint- the very overt sign of weakness and decline that he abhors. Time waits for no man, but this man waits for Alexander. Sighing exaggeratedly to communicate his impatience, George sneaks another peak at the names of those who have recently passed on to the other side.

Every day he reluctantly reads these blasted names from the local paper to his brother, but every day his eyes are curiously, and with trepidation, dragged to the bottom right of the page. 'Yule' is the name he is looking for. Angela Jane Yule. Well Yule, that was her maiden name, she might be married now. He thought she was the key to his happy future. He doesn't know if she's married now and doesn't wish to know either. Ever since she had left him, he has made a concerted effort to blot the memories that he shared with her out of his mind, but somehow he can't, he is powerless to stop them. He knows nothing of her life now, but he once knew everything, every minute detail a man would covet about the woman he loves.

Now every day he ponders that he might learn of her conclusion. Five years his elder she'll be in her mid-seventies now and it has been decades since the seminal letter she left on their kitchen table marked their last point of contact. Never a day goes past without George considering what might have been, how his life might have panned out had he chosen a life on the road with her; a fresh start over his brother in his hour of greatest need.

Each and every day since she closed the door on him for the last time, he looks at the letter that he keeps in the recesses of his tattered brown leather wallet. Only George and she who penned it know of its existence or have read its content. The words are imprinted on his brain even more clearly than the faded black ink on starched paper which is stained like milk coffee. He could quote the 236 words verbatim and every rereading of it feels like a gut wrenching knee to the midriff:

*01/07/1972*

*Dear George,*

*It is through tears and the most enormous feeling of regret imaginable that I feel compelled to write these words. Please do not think that this is a decision I have taken lightly. I can assure you with all my heart that it isn't, but it is one that I have to do for myself. I have given you the choice to come with me, but you have elected to stay and look after your brother and that is something I cannot and will not have a go at you for- he is family and needs you now more than ever and it is right that you cannot leave him on his own and break his heart further.*

*As you know, this chance for me to move to London is a once in a lifetime and I have to take it. I have to pursue my career and being in Dundee won't allow me to do that. It is not too late for you to change your mind though George, my train leaves at 11.00 tonight, it's the overnight train to Kings Cross. If you have a change of heart and want to come with me you can meet me on the platform.*

*If you are not there, I will accept that we are over and we'll have to sever contact because I won't settle there if we write to each other. I have to set up a new life down there with or without you. I admire your loyalty to Eck and he needs you now and I will understand whatever decision you make and will always love you. Please take care of yourself and that brother of yours and perhaps one day we can be back together again where we truly belong.*

*Your best friend and loving fiancé. Forever yours.*

*Angie.*

George never made that train. He wanted desperately to do so, but his loyalties ultimately lay with his bloodline. Not a day passes, though, when he does not think of that letter or when his eyes don't well up as he considers how his life would have changed forever-most probably for the better . She was the love of his life and he's never replaced her, never tried to, never wanted to, never had a single iota of desire to. That day was seminal, the day his life was to change forever, the day that he lost his liberation and became tied forever to the man he was born only minutes after, a man who he loves and felt a gnawing responsibility for, despite the despair he often felt for him.

For five blissful years Angela's relationship with George was unshakable, they formed an unbreakable bond through a compelling physical attraction and a mutual understanding of each other's viewpoint and beliefs. For the final year of their relationship they co-habited in George's council house in the Kirkton area of Dundee, provoking disdainful whispers and much head shaking from many in the predominantly Roman Catholic community. But Angela and George were cut from the same cloth; they were non conformists who care little for what they saw as stuffy conservative views and ignored the oft spouted belief that they were ' living in sin'. They shared working class values and a desire to make the most of the cards they had been dealt. While George was working shifts on the production line in NCR, Angela was a dressmaker and designer with a small independent fabric shop on the Perth Road, a job she undertook with remarkable passion and diligence. She, like George, was small in height but strong of heart and of stature with a personality and caustic wit that George adored. Angela had a thick main of dark, curly hair which contrasted with her piercing emerald green eyes, which formed the centrepiece of a very pleasantly pretty face.

Eight months before Angela absconded, George's romantic side led him to propose under the moonlit bandstand on Dundee Riverside's Magdalen Green, which lies ironically close to the home in which he now reluctantly resides. Weeping tears of undiluted joy, she accepted immediately and the prosperous pair promised each other that nothing would stand in their way- they were made to be after all, that is what they had told each other nearly every day since they met. But fate soon intervened and the death of George's mother contrived to create a double disaster that was to befall his twin brother and prove a catalyst for a series of events so bizarre and unfortunate that they would ultimately lead to their enforced separation- a riftless split that looks unlikely ever to be repaired.

' Well, that's me ready to go then George. Are you ready to go now by any chance? You always keep me waiting around. I'll tell you, punctuality is certainly not one of your stronger points, in fact you could learn a thing or two from me in that respect. I can get ready before you, even with my brittle bones and my rheumatism and my chronic back ache, not to mention my insomnia or the migraines. Quite remarkable really, ' Alexander says while fumbling in his pockets for his keys and looking over his brother's shoulder towards the door.

George thinks he tells him to piss off, but he can't be sure.

# 8

# FUNERAL

Walking out of the Riverview Nursing and Retirement Home, George casts his critical gaze over the communal area that he rarely attends. In the corner is Lizzie, a woman so riddled with Alzheimer's Disease that she can't recall even her own name, the remainder of what life she has left passing in an undignified haze of forgetfulness. Next to her is Joe, an amusing old fellow who, in the absence of anyone else to play against, is practising how to get a four move check mate on himself. Then there's Eddie, an octogenarian who sits with a tartan rug over his knees even in the height of summer and bases his entire day's activities around the appearance of the Countdown conundrum. George nods in disapproval and grunts something indecipherable, before following Alexander's loping stride through the front door and out into the gravelly car park.

With Alexander at the wheel, their 16 year old brown Austin Allegro clunks and creaks slowly into the street that leads down towards Downfield South Church, the worn brake pads screaming and screeching to be changed. As the exhaust pipe coughs infectiously, the brothers look like something from the Whacky Races; Alexander stooping his head over the steering wheel as George just about manages to peer a scowl over the dusty dashboard. Outside, the meek sun has been permanently kidnapped by a threatening cloud which cast a gloomy shadow over the area's grey streets. This is summer, but it is a wintery landscape outside. In the passenger's seat, George surveys the decaying tenement houses that surround him with their darkened windows. Plastic bins overflowing with decrepit cardboard and crushed cans stand guard at the front doors, waiting untidily to be spruced up. Flies feast like gannets on a half-eaten chicken leg and the debris from a Chinese take away skulks in the wind as a squawking seagull stalks above, circling around its prey like a mugger waiting for his moment to pounce on the vulnerable. Outside a lonely row of shops a child no older than six years of age is dragged from the pavement by a vicious looking dog that's nearly twice his weight, but has double the number of teeth. It barks angrily as Alexander toots his horn before it squats threateningly on the unkempt weedy area of grassland, bearing its fangs before emptying the contents of its bladder under a single skeletal tree. This is urban desolation and George shakes his head, but he shakes it with regret not anger. This used to be his kind of place. Not the type of area that he was brought up in, but the type of council house estate that he has once lived in and thought was his future- until Alexander's circumstances dictated otherwise. Looking around the tattered clothing hanging from washing lines and the green paint work peeling from the railings, George inwardly decries the neglect this place has been treated with, the disdain for its people from outside and within. It is now a place where people are frightened to tread after nightfall, where drugs are pedalled openly on the streets and children play around the broken syringes while raking the bins for scraps of food to eat. This, to him, should be a place with working class values, where community spirit flies in the place of difficult times through graft and hard work, where people worked to earn their corn in difficult circumstances. The children of these streets were once, like he was, fodder for the factories, generations of families working in Dundee's manufacturing industries. But now the jobs have headed east and the motivation of many has been sieved away. It's a shell of the place where he used to live, the place where he thought he'd spend his life with the woman he loved, raising the family he wanted so badly. His dream died, so has this place. How he hankers for the times when his life meant something to someone and to himself. He doesn't blame Alexander,

33

he was just helping him at his lowest ebb as any brother would.

' I'll just pull in here George,' says Alexander, ' at least I'll be able to see it from the church. I wouldn't want any of those feral children to damage it while we are in paying our respects to James. I'm not sure how I will manage the walk though George, I mean my rheumatism is really playing up today and this back of mine is giving me intolerable jip.'

George hates the way his brother's Alexander side comes out. You can take Eck out of the Alexander, but you can't take Alexander out of the Eck. And after all is said and done, he is Eck- a Dundee boy like him, but his life on the other side of the track with a silver spoon rammed down his gob has cultivated this snobbish side to him that riles George to the core of his being.

' You ought tae mind what side yir bread is buttered on Eck. Just because these poor bastards were no given the same chance at education as you were, doesnae give yi the right tae slag them off,' George snaps back, 'and remember I wisnae given the chances that you were and used to live in a council scheme like this tae, but look at the way it's turned. These folk are looked on like shit, schemers as you call them. What chance have they got? They're lost tae society, nae hopers with nae futures cos people like you have attitudes like that. '

It is rare for George to speak in so many words, he is a man of very few, but his impassioned sentiments barely register with Alexander. Clattering the undercarriage against the steep street crib, he reverses his rusted brown car into a space on double yellow lines just yards from the front door.

' You shouldnae be allowed on the road, yir too auld. There should be a test fir folk your age. Yir mare dangerous than the kids. Now are yi sure yi will manage this walk? It must be all of 20 yards after all,' George barks venomously.

' Keep your voice down George, this is a funeral we are going to would you ever remember? It is about time that you started treating these occasions with the level of dignity that befits them instead of acting like a petulant little child.   And, by the way, now you mention it, you would be wise to consider that you are extremely lucky I can drive because how would you get around without me? I won't be driving for much longer if my eyes get any worse than they are now and then you will really be sorry. In fact I must book in for an appointment with the optician the week after next- assuming that we are not booked up with friends' funerals that is. I am pretty sure it is a problem with my cataracts. '

' There's fuck all wrang we yir eyes and I can easy get the bus, in fact eh actually prefer it that way, at least I wouldnae hae tae put up wi your drivel every minute o' the day. I'm no an invalid yi ken. Now let's get in there and get this fucking thing oot the road. What are we dain' here anyway? We barely even ken this poor bugger, especially you,' George seethes.

' You cannot swear like that outside a place of worship. This is your, I mean our, old friend's funeral we are going to remember. Goodness, gracious me. I mean, what on earth would Jimmy say if he could hear you speaking about his funeral like that?' Alexander replies in forced incredulity.

' I'll tell you what he would really say, he'd say ' who the fuck are these two stupid lookin' idiots and what the fuck are they doin' at meh funeral? Eh've no spoken to him fir aboot 50 years and as for his stupid lookin' brother, eh only met him once in meh life and even that was once too often.…'

Alexander can only shake his head and tactically ignore his brother's volcanic ire. He knows it is best to stand back and let the fire die out rather than try to intervene and pour petrol on the smoldering flames. Lifting his long limbs under the steering wheel, he plants his size 14 polished brown brogues on the pavement and pushes himself upright, grabbing onto the back that he'd forgotten was causing him pain. ' Oh, I'll be next at this rate, it'll be my funeral you are coming to George, my body is giving up on me and I can't say that I blame it after all it has been put through.'

' Chance will be a fine thing,' George mutters inaudibly as he struggles out of the car, his left hand pushing down heavily on his walking stick to bring himself as upright as his creaking limbs will allow.

'Oh hurry along George, we're late enough as it is,' Alexander tuts while striding ahead of his brother's shuffling gait. George seethes, but saves his retort for a time and a place where taking the Lord's name in vain won't be so frowned upon from above. George limps heavily and Alexander walks freely towards the domineering church door which has been painted in questionable distaste in a gaudy bright red colour. As Alexander squeezes the door ajar the sombre, nervous wheeze of the church organ fills the air and they quietly enter.

'I think I'll try to get a seat as close to the front as possible George, it's only right that I should be close to the family in case they need a shoulder to cry on,' Alexander whispers in full earnest as he uses his long neck to peer like a periscope over the grieving heads of the congregation in an effort to locate a seat as close to the minister's pew as their unpunctual arrival will facilitate.

' You'll dae nothin o the sort,' George replies a little more audibly than he had truly intended, grabbing his brother by the sleeve of his suit.

' Now sit yir stupid backside doon here and stop makin' even mare o' a fool of us than you already are,' George tones his voice down to a notch above a whisper, forcibly grabbing the cuff of his brother's overcoat and dragging him into the empty pew in the furthermost bowels of the church where he believes their tenuous link to the family Brown merits. Their distant positioning is much to Alexander's chagrin and he heaves a protesting sigh which mirrors the organist's pedalling wheeze. The brothers' late entrance has turned a few inquisitive heads and an elderly couple seated two rows in front trade nudges and glances before exchanging shoulder shrugs and shaking heads.

' I thought it would be standing room only given how popular Jimmy was, but it's a fair gathering nonetheless,' Alexander says cupping his words quietly, he thinks, into his brother's ear.

'Shhhh, flammin' keep it doon Eck for God's sake. The minister's trying tae start the bloody service and you are still prattling on aboot nothin'. You'll get us thrown oot o here ya daft get,' George whispers angrily.

' Ok, calm down George, you're doing your blood pressure no good at all by acting like this. It will be higher even than mine at this rate- if that is even possible. And how many times have I told you, my name is Alexander not Eck, especially here in church. And also, do not take the Lord's name in vain, especially here in the church. So that's both my name and the Lord's you've insulted in one sentence,' Alexander whispers earnestly.

As the minister's head appears above the parapet, Alexander turns the volume up on the hearing aid on his right ear and down on his left. Neither action has any effect because it is actually turned off. He cocks his head in the direction of the front of the church and can see George's lips moving aggressively out of the corner of his left eye but is blissfully ignorant to its content. At a guess, he imagines, it might contain several words with four letters, the majority of which will begin with either the letter 'f' or the letter 'c'. He's heard it all too frequently blaring through his hearing aid.

Dressed in regulation pristine white dog collar and coal black sweater, the minister is a man of around 60 years who is positively hirsute

37

with a generous helping of wispy grey hair, well-trimmed beard and a pair of penny round spectacles perched precariously just below the bridge of his nose. He stands authoritatively with his hands grabbing the sides of the lectern, the whites of his knuckles peeping through as his dark eyes narrow over the top of his glasses and towards the pair of feuding siblings at the back of the church. They quickly settle to his glance.

' Ladies and gentlemen, please remain seated,' he says loudly clearing a frog from his throat with a raspy, echoing cough. He begins: ' We are gathered here today to celebrate the life of the fondly remembered Mr. James Brown. Please remain seated congregation,' he encourages as he spots Alexander lurching to his feet at the back of the church to gain a more superior view.

'A few words on the dearly departed. James died on Wed June 24, 2013. As we remember him, our sympathy and prayers go out to the family and friends that he left behind, especially his wife and their two children, along with their families, grandchildren and all the huge number of close friends who have kindly gathered here for this service today,' Alexander nods his head slowly and purses his lips in agreement, inching forward in his seat and turning his right hearing aid      further      in      the      direction      of      the      sermon.

'They all grieve in a special way today before the loving God of Heaven here at Downfield Church, in the city of Dundee that meant so terribly much to James, or Jimmy as all his family and friends knew him as, he was truly a man after God's own heart and a person who inspired others whilst giving all whom he met the ultimate respect that he believed everyone deserved,' the minister says turning his head upwards towards the heavens then down to Jimmy Brown's family.

' I couldn't agree more with those words,' Alexander whispers, dabbing a dribbling  crocodile tear from his eye with a faded white handkerchief which bears the initials A.P.in the corner in blue embroidered writing. George's blood boils and babbles around his protruding veins but he elects to look staunchly ahead, tuning in intensely with the rest of the congregation.

' Paul speaks of Death in 1 Corinthians 15 as the last enemy to be defeated. And this enemy brings sorrow and suffering in its wake, and it can leave a hole within our stomachs and hearts -- within our soul -- that nothing can seem to fill. And yet as we turn to the gospels, we take heart that Jesus overcame death and resurrected to life, the same life he promises to those who believe in him. In the Gospel of John, Jesus says "I am the Resurrection and the Life. He who believes in me shall live, even if he dies, and everyone who lives and believes in me shall never die.' Gentle sobbing can be heard in pockets around the church and strong armed men place comforting arms around their wives and children's shoulders. Meanwhile at the back of the church Alexander is turning slowly but surely into an inconsolable wreck, drawing fleeting glances from the deceased's family and friends who turn to see from where the caterwaul wailing noises are emitting.

' It's just so, so dreadfully upsetting George,' Alexander gargles through the tears and the lump he has worked to create in his own throat, ' It is just so terribly, awfully upsetting.'

Standing slightly on his tip toes, the minister continues, fixing his gaze on Alexander in the back row, who is now approaching emotional apoplexy. George begins the process of detachment as he inches further away from him using his walking stick to push his ailing body along the smooth wooden seating, but in doing so he accidently clangs it against the metal radiator beneath his feet, drawing incongruous tuts from others in the congregation, particularly his brother.

'And yet, there is still that hole, and pain and grief is normal. It's natural. It's OK to cry. It's OK to mourn and remember,' the minister urges, offering a pitying nod in Alexander's direction. ' But it's OK to laugh, as well. We must learn to focus on the good times and not allow the bad to sap our souls. Please consider how Jimmy would have liked you to celebrate his passing and take your lead from a friend so sadly departed.'

Through his tears, which are now flowing like an uncontrollable babbling brook, Alexander, following the minister to his exact word, puts his hand over his mouth to stifle a fake laugh, as if his memory bank has just recalled a hilarious anecdote from a past together that barely existed. George is now sitting over three feet from his brother as heads begin to turn in their direction with increasing regularity.

' But that pain is something we need comfort for. And the only one who can truly sustain and comfort us for the long haul and for eternity is our Heavenly Father. So I'm going to lead us in prayer at this time, and at the appropriate time, I'm going to ask you to join in the Lord's Prayer, and when you do, please use the words "debts" and "debtors." Please congregation, be standing.'

The congregation stands as one. ' Our father who art in heaven,' Alexander staggers to his feet barely able to hold himself upright. ' Hallowed be they name,' George shuffles further along the pew. 'Thy Kingdom come, thy will be done on earth as it is in heaven,' George shuffles towards the exit, the sound of his walking stick clicking on the wooden floor drowned out by the congregations' recital. ' Give us this day, the daily bread and forgive us our debts as we forgive our debtors,' Alexander's tears have suddenly dried, he stands open jawed watching his brother depart the church. ' Lead us not into temptation, but deliver us from evil for thine is the Kingdom, the power and the glory, forever and ever Amen.' The crowd repeat Amen in heartfelt unison, Alexander flees for the exit to confront George.

Outside the church, George is incandescent with rage, his stocky frame squatting in pent up fury, hauling at the door handle on the passenger's side of his embarrassing sibling's ramshackle car as Alexander charges out of the church in hot pursuit.

' George, what on earth are you doing, the service is still going on. You can't just leave like that. I know you're upset, I am too, but we have to pay our respects,' says Alexander, whose powers of emotional recovery have stood up remarkably to their hasty retreat.

' Upset? Fucking right em upset! But, em no upset aboot Jimmy fuckin' Broon, eh barely even ken the poor bugger, but em fuckin upset alright, I'll tell yi that fir nothing,' George blasts in unkempt fury.

' Please George, try not to swear outside the church. You seem angry, what's wrong?' replies Alexander as he stretches an arm out towards his brother.

' What's wrong?!' George is shouting now, after all he is neither inclined to matiness nor afraid of a snarl. ' I'll tell you what's fucking wrong. It's you that's wrong Eck, you are a fuckin embarrassment, blubberin' and greetin' like a wee bubbly bairn aboot a guy you dinnae even ken. You are making a total show o' us in front o' the entire congregation. Everyone's lookin' around thinkin', 'who the fuck are these clowns at the back of the church wailing like wounded dogs. It's a pure embarrassment, a total beamer and em no putting up with it any longer,' he yanks at the car door handle again, a smattering of rust dropping to the ground as he repeats the motion. ' Open it!' he screams.

' George, would you keep your voice down and stop swearing in front of the church. Have some respect and the name's Alexander remember.'

' Calm down?!' George rants, aiming a kick at the car's front wheel,

41

before whacking it with his walking stick. His face has turned a deep scarlet shade. ' You have seen nothing yet! Now get this car open right noo, we're going back tae that fuckin' home you've prisoned me in.'

Alexander stands ashen faced, his head drooped in all the anguished hurt of a puppy dog denied of his morning feed. He fumbles in his pocket for his initialed handkerchief which is sopping with overuse. ' You know how difficult I find these services George. You know that after all I have been through. This is so, so difficult for me, it really is and I would have thought that you of all people would at least understand and afford me just a little sympathy,' Alexander mopes in search of sympathy.

' Difficult? Difficult?! If this is difficult fir you, then it is your ain fault. It is you and you alone who chooses to put yersel' through this every other day. You're the bugger who begs me to go we him tae these things every other day so dinnae give me your shite. You met Jimmy Broon once in your life. Now you are sittin' at the back of his funeral service greetin' like a wee bairn as if he was the best friend that you had ever met in yir life, ' barks George unrepentantly.

' But it's Jimmy's family I feel for George, did you see how upset they were? They were inconsolable. We know what it is like to lose family close to us don't we? I so wish that we had more family around us, people we are close to, people to love us and miss us if we were gone. Who would I have at my funeral if I was to die George? You. You and who else? Maybe Nurse Mabel and a few of the chess team from Riverview Nursing and Retirement Home, but apart from that, who? Nobody. Nobody at all,' Alexander wails.

Battle against it as he might, it is at moments like these that George's resolve diminishes and his default of sympathetic pity intervenes. Scuffing his feet back onto the stone kerb, he tries to avoid looking at Alexander, he can paint an accurate illustration of his face in his mind without even seeing it. He knows that, deep down, the tears are exaggerated but full of a genuine mixture of upset and remorse inspired by the past. He knows that his features display heartfelt hurt and mindboggling loneliness. Yes, he doesn't know Jimmy Brown from the next man on the street, but he can empathise with his family. He can share their feelings of pain and distress, that nagging sore that loss brings, the scab that never quite heals. As usual, those tumbling thoughts of the difficulties of the past encourage him to relent somewhat.

' Listen here,' says George, his voice softening slightly from its natural gruff tone, ' We'll wait on the family and friends coming oot the church after the ceremony, we'll see if there are any faces we ken fae the past. Now here, take this hanky and clean that daft puss of yours up, yi look a right state.' He lifts his hand to pat his brother on the back, but stops short, he finds expressing his sympathy in such gestures difficult. Alexander takes the handkerchief and dabs his eyes from beneath the rims of his glasses, the top of the frames deflecting off his heavy grey, waspish eyebrows.

'Thanks very much George,' he replies regaining his composure. ' That means a lot to me and so do you. You know that don't you? I know I am not the easiest man to contend with all the time, but I really do appreciate what you do for me.'

George purses his lips together and just about stops himself from nodding.

# 9

## THE PAST AWAKES

The congregation files mournfully out into the church yard to the faint calling of 'The Lord's My Shepherd' which is interspersed by rhythmic sound of somber footsteps slowly crunching on the pebbled surface. Grief stricken friends trade handshakes and silently empathetic nods as whispered pleasantries, smiles and anecdotes are respectfully exchanged by mourners reunited through a shared loss.

George and Alexander stand at the corner of the yard, the difference in their heights accentuated by their shifting awkwardness. Suddenly from out of the dark crowd appears a face familiar to one of the brothers. His countenance is largely hidden by brown national health glasses and his body slightly is frail and emaciated, but George recognises that protruding jawline straight away.

' Geordie Pace, well eh never. It must be whit, 55 years?' the old man's voice falters slightly as he introduces himself with an extended wrinkled hand and a whistling lilt. There was a rogue like quality to his voice that George recognised immediately despite it being more than half a century since the last time he had heard it.

Turning to put a face to a voice, there is an immediate recognition that flashes before him like, ' Alan Patterson, eh'll tell yi what you have nae changed a bit. I'd recognize that jaw anywhere! How are you doin'? Long, long, long time no see. You still eatin' the cow pies?' George says jauntily, temporarily forgetting the potential embarrassment that being spotted at the funeral of someone he hardly knew could bring.

' Eh, good one! I've been stuck we this jaw ah me life, even meh mother called me Desperate Dan! It's bad when even yir ain mother takes the piss oot the way that you look! Never mind a puss only a mother would love, this is a puss even meh mother doesn't love!' Alan replies self mockingly, the two men slipping so naturally into dressing room style banter it is as if they hadn't spent a minute apart, never mind decades.

' So how are yi anyway? All joking aside yir looking well, are yi feelin' well too?' asked George.

' Eh no bad Geordie, eh. Meh God, I think we were playin' together for the Lochee Harp at Beechwood Park the last time eh saw you, we used to be the best of mates, eh thought you'd just disappeared off the face of the earth. Here one minute, gone the next. Terrible shame on Broony eh? Eh didnae realise you kent him well,' says Alan probingly.

' Well, eh, I eh, I ken him aright,' George flusters and fumbles trying to find his words, 'Eh used to play with him at the Downfield. No fir long right enough, but eh saw the announcement in the Courier and it struck a wee bit of a chord wi me so I thought I'd just come along and show meh respects. He was a right good lad, a good player tae,' George says, impressing himself with the composure he manages to maintain.

The handshake turns to a brief man hug, it's well out of George's comfort zone for his personal space to be invaded but there is a genuine rapport between the two men, an undeniable outpouring of happiness. Alan is the sort of man that George enjoys spending time with; down to earth, working class and humble with the ability to tease and 'take the piss' in the name of mirth. Alexander, meanwhile, cuts an awkward figure a couple of yards adrift of the reuniting pair. He is quietly seething. 'This is what I come to these funerals for- to meet people, to mingle to reacquaint myself with people from the past, to find popularity,' he thinks to himself, struggling to contain a cough to encourage them to at least acknowledge his presence in their company, ' He didn't even want to come, said he didn't know Jimmy Brown and here he is stealing my thunder. I'm the one who's upset after all,' he muses inwardly.

' That is very good of yi. Eh there are loads o the fitba boys here, will be good to catch up we them after. Are you going back to the wake for a pint and a bowl of soup? Eh cannae mind where the minister said it is, eh think it's just doon the road though,' says Alan, checking his watch.

Before George can answer, his brother interjects keenly to make his presence felt, ' Soup and sandwiches at Doc Stewarts it said in the newspaper. Unless it's changed since then. I didn't hear the end of the ceremony, I was too upset to hear. I'm Alexander by the way. Alexander Pace, George's brother. Twin brother in fact. I am very pleased to meet you. I'm not sure I caught your name right, it is Alan isn't it?' he says extending his thin hand, ' George always forgets his manners and never introduces me to anyone. Anyone would think he's embarrassed of his own brother,' he adds half in joke, entirely in earnest.

Shaking George's hand firmly, Alan squints at Alexander, the cogs in his head whirling in a desperate effort to remind himself where he has seen his face before.

'Pleased to meet you,' Alan smiles and loosens the firm grip he has taken on Alexander's hand, ' You have a very familiar face, have I met you before somewhere? Funny enough, I remember George having a twin brother, but the name's not familiar to me. '

' That's because his name isnae Alexander, it's Eck or Ecky. He likes to pretend he is all posh these days,' George interjects mimicking a snooty accent, twice flicking the nib of his nose skyward with his right index finger.

' Tosh and piffle,' Alexander says, his word choice doing little to dispel George's accusation. 'Do not listen to him. My name's Alexander. I'm not sure where we've met before, maybe the football I would say. I played a bit as well you know, before all the injuries set in,' Alexander replies pointing to various limbs and body parts.

' Eh, he played once as a sub and was worse than a man doon,' jokes George raising his eyes to the heavens. ' The only reason he got a game was because stumpy no legs and blind man buff were unavailable! He's the only player in the Downfield's history ever to be taken off when we had nae subs to replace him with, he was walking aboot too faird tae tackle anyone, claimin' tae be injured and runnin' away fae the ball like a wee lassie. After that game anyone who we thought was faking an injury was called an 'Ecky Pace.' George and Alan share a stifled laugh, aware that an outright chortle wouldn't exactly be befitting of the solemn situation. For George, it's like the dressing room banter he used to enjoy so much, he is in his comfort zone speaking to a 'normal' person who enjoys the cut of his jib. Not like the chess team at the nursing home who, George believes, have all the sense of humour of a morgue dweller. Giggling mutedly George becomes aware of how little he has laughed in the past few years, how much he has missed that feeling of losing your inhibitions, enjoying yourself. There is something about George's default look that doesn't comfortably host a laugh and a smile, when his face lights up it draws an almost sympathetic response. He knows he should do it much more often, but when does he ever get the chance? Not with  the chess mob that is for certain.

' Yeah, very funny George, you two ought to remember where you are and show a little bit of respect for James and his family,' Alexander tuts- he hates being the butt of his brother's gags especially in front of someone he believes he has never previously met.

Still smirking like a scolded school boy, Alan suddenly clicks his fingers and waggles his index finger three times in Alexander's direction, ' I've got it now, it has just come to me' he says knowingly nodding his head, ' You're Ecky Pace. Right enough, I am sure that you used to go we a lassie eh kent. Now what wis her name…..' Alan pauses to consider, rubbing his temple as if to encourage lost memories to return.

Meantime, George looks at Alexander whose face resembles a ghost who has just seen a ghost; a look of abject terror that has drained his visage of all its blood. He knows exactly what is coming and there is nothing he can do to prevent the words flowing from his mouth.

George tries desperately to interject, attempting to shunt the topic on a tangent to prevent the inevitable distress he knows is marching unabated in his direction. ' So, will we head on doon to Doc Stewarts, time is getting away from….'

' Eh've got it, eh've got it!,' Alan said excitedly cajoling memories long since forgotten, ' Eh knew I knew your face fae somewhere. You used to go out with a girl I was at school with. Her name was Mary, Mary Farrelly eh think. Eh, that wis her name wasn't it? Mary Farrelly! She was a wee cracker, you lucky devil. Everybody in the school used to fancy her,' he continued apace.

In a heartbeat Alexander takes on the appearance of someone who's just been informed that his mother's been killed in a freak yachting accident. He visibly wilts, his face instantaneously draining of what semblance of colour it had retained. Alan's apparently throw away remark has acted like a stake in Alexander's heart.

' Sorry, I've just come over a little faint all of a sudden,' Alexander stammers, his voice has risen a couple of octaves, 'I'll need to sit down for a minute. George, give me that walking stick.' Grabbing his brother's walking aid, he staggers absent footedly over to a decaying wooden chair which sits neglected under the church's jutting canopy. He perches himself on the edge of the chair, inhaling exaggeratedly, clutching at his chest as he rest his elbows on his elongated limbs. He rubs his forehead with his thumb and fore finger before opening the top button of his shirt, loosening his burgundy tie to allow air to cool off a pool of sweat that has appeared on his gullet.

' Bloody hell Geordie, is he alright? Was it something eh said? Did eh say something tae upset him,' Alan whispers to George, looking on agog as Alexander feeds his ravenous lungs with enormous intakes of oxygen.

' Eh it's nae bother. That name's just a no go for him, it hasnae been uttered to him in years. She nearly ruined the pair bugger's life. Sorry, she did ruin his life and basically ruined mine tae. I'll tell yi all aboot it over a pint later if I get the chance. Just give him a minute, he'll be alright.' George replies tugging on Alan's shirt sleeve to prevent him going over to check on Alexander's welfare.

' Crikey me, it must be bad. I thought he'd seen a ghost for a second. His puss just drained of colour. Eh wis just jokin' with him tae, eh would never have mentioned her name if I knew better, ' Alan says, his face suddenly etched with concern.

' He may well have seen a ghost, eh'll just see if he's ok,' says George inching intrepidly over to see his brother. ' You ok Eck? Come on dinnae worry aboot it. He didnae mean tae upset you,' his voice taking on an unusually sympathetic tone. ' Come on, let's get yi a stiff drink doon at Doc Stewarts.'

' Oh George, my heart is pounding, I'm feeling weak as a straw. This is no good for my weak heart or my high blood pressure. I'm going to have to go back to the home and see Nurse Mabel,' he whimpers clutching his chest with his trembling right hand. ' You go ahead to the wake George, I'm not able or fit for it now. Give my regards to the Brown family and apologise for the fact that I never made it down,' Alexander says dragging his trembling body around.

George masks a frown, 'They dinna even ken him so it's no as if they'll miss him,' he thinks to himself hoping that he hasn't vocalised his feelings. ' Are you sure yir aright tae drive Eck? Do yi want me tae come with yi,' George says holding his brother's thin right forearm to help him towards the car.

' No, it's ok now you go ahead George. You know me, I'll be just fine. I'll take some pills when I get back to the home and Nurse Mabel will take care of me. You go and represent our family at the pub.'

And with that, Alexander stumbles into the Alegro , softly clatters the rusted door closed and drives raggedly into the distance, almost taking some of the mourners with him as he goes.

' So that's the brother,' George sighs looking sideways at Alan whose look of bemusement paints a comical picture. ' He is honestly a great man, but he is also the bane of meh fucking life,' George says shaking his head.

' Come on Georgdie, let's get a pint and you can tell me all aboot it. You look like yi need a stiff one,' Alan replies shaking his head sympathetically in union.

' Eh need mare than one that's for sure.'



Having steered clear of too many pleasantries with the family Brown, George Pace strokes clear the condensation from his pint glass and takes a frothy gulp of lager, exhaling in satisfaction as the fluid courses its way through his bloodstream. Sitting beside him at a table for two in one of the nooks in Doc Stewart's public house, Alan Patterson nurses a pint of Guinness and pours a dash of water into his malt whisky chaser, the ice cubes clinking against the side of the glass as the liquid turns a treacly amber colour.

George looks around himself and takes a moment to appreciate how everyone in the room has been dragged together through grief. There's a camaraderie he's missed desperately, a shared empathy that drags people together. Though he feels like a legal alien in the room, he still feels a liberation and belonging. The drinks bring a buzz to a congregation which is sharing memories, provoking laughs and tears in equal measure. He notes the coming together of old friends and briefly yearns for the chance to turn back the clock, to relive the years he has dedicated to someone else in exchange for his own social happiness.

Consuming a large gulp of his scantly diluted whisky, Alan's mouth turns the amber to a glassy yellow as he breaks the brief silence, ' It's a great turn oot fir Jimmy eh? He deserved it, he was a great lad. Never harmed a flea.'

' Aye, he'll be a miss alright, ' says George vaguely, staring out the window to avoid further inquisition from Alan about his near non-existent relationship with the late Jimmy Broon.

' So, the brother. Tell me aboot him. You twa are no exactly twa pees in a pod! He sure reacted badly when he mentioned that Mary lassie he used to go oot we! So what happened, she was a lawyer wis she? ' Alan probed.

' How long have we got?' asks George taking a large gulp from his pint.

' Well last time eh looked eh never had much in meh diary. Meh daughter's comin' aroond the night to make meh tea, but that's no 'til six so I've got of plenty time,' Alan replies encouraging his old friend to share his thoughts with him.

' You have a daughter? How old is she?' George asks.

' I've two, they're 38 and 41, lovely lassies, Bella and Jane. Five grandbairns too, they're meh life noo. I absolutely dote on them so I do. I'm on my own now though, the missus died eight years ago. It was a real blow to me, I never thought I'd survive it. So, unfortunately Geordie, meh diary is fairly sparse this weather, so eh have all the time in the world tae listen, I'm all ears,' he said adding the creases of a haunted smile to his craggy features. 'But the grandkids are my life noo, they helped make it easier,' Alan confides, his face the perfect amalgamation of sorrow and pride.

' I'm sorry tae hear that, Alan. Aboot the missus I mean. Must be lovely tae have the grandkids around though,' George replies sincerely, desperately trying to stop his mind to drifting to the regrets of his past. He knows what's coming next though...

' Thanks George, I really miss her pal. What aboot you? Wife? Bairns? Grandbairns?'

' No none of the above unfortunately. Nae family at all- except for the brother. But that's another story. Well it's kind of another story,' he says hurriedly trying to dismiss the question out of hand.

Alan is good enough to take the hint and alters the subject, but only slightly, ' So, go on then Geordie, tell me aboot the brother,' he urges. ' That was very strange outside the kirk, eh think eh struck a raw nerve beh mentioning that lassie Mary's name.'

' That's just aboot the understatement of the last twa millenniums. Now let me get yi another drink, you will need it fir this. Same again?'

Flagging down the somber looking waitress, George orders another round – a pint of lager for himself and a pint of the black stuff with a whisky and water for Alan- and sets about relating his tale. It's a story that has gone around in his head a million times, but one that he has rarely communicated to anyone. Though Alan Patterson could hardly be described as a close, lifelong friend, there is something about the situation that George finds himself in that is encouraging loose lips.

 It is a long time since George has been free of the burden of Alexander, been able to talk to a peer without his lanky brother lurking over his shoulder vetting his every uttering. The surroundings of the pub encourages relaxation in his mind and body, he feels that Alan is a man of similar standing and values as he is, a working class man he can talk to without feeling judged or corrected.

Alan sits back in his bar chair, sips from his pint and opens his ears to his reunited friend. George takes a huge gulp of his pint, a heavy intake of the musty bar room oxygen and tells his tale to Alan, his words       paraphrased       to       suit       a       wider       audience:


'It's fair to say that, for twins, me and Eck lived fairly separate lives growing up. We were never the type of twin brothers that you read about who never spent a second apart and have this almost telepathic relationship with each other, it just wasn't like that in our house. It was mainly mum who made it that way, she urged us down different paths from an early age and saw Eck as the brains and me as the brawn. Dad kind of agreed, but he saw more of himself in me and didn't complain much about anything mum said or did really, mainly to keep the peace. But, despite the fact that we were set off on different tracks ( I saw it like two trains travelling in the same direction but headed for different destinations- if Eck was the Orient Express, I was the Stevenson Steam engine) there was an empathy between us, a silent closeness that would not be obvious on the surface. When push came to shove we would look out for each other, scratch each other's backs. Nothing would hurt me more than seeing Eck troubled or upset, that's true to this day and that's perhaps been my biggest failing in life, if you could call it a failing.

We grew up in fairly average surroundings, a two bedroom tenement in the west end of Dundee with a communal outside toilet and washroom, a shared garden with a wooden fence that ran down between the houses and a damp wooden shed at the bottom where we used to set up a den as kids. It was hardly paradise but we were happy enough and never knew any better. I never thought mum was too happy there though, she was a teacher who gave it up to bring up me and Eck and look after the house while dad was the bread winner at the NCR factory. Looking back at it now, she was a bit snobbish that way. Dad never made too much money but we always had food on the table and were treated well at Christmas and birthdays. I always thought mum felt she could be doing better than what we had, that her life lacked intellectual challenge and the trappings she felt she could provide if she had gone to work rather than mind the house.

Eck and I always shared a room growing up, there was hardly enough room in there to swing a mouse never mind a cat, but while we bickered and fought like any other brothers do we generally got on well and treated each other a bit better than ok. We were different though, we looked different and we liked different things. He was always taller than me and skinnier, though he never beat me in a scrap. And while I had pictures of my favourite Scotland or Dundee football players on the wall, he would have scientists and historians whose names I couldn't even pronounce. Dad would take us to the football every Saturday- Dens one week to see Dundee, Tannadice the next to see United, but Eck had hardly any interest. While dad had me on his shoulders so I could see the action better, Eck would be reading the 'Famous Five' or staring at the back of some old guy's knees. It just wasn't his thing.

Our differences were really highlighted at school, everything's exaggerated in that setting anyway. Eck was a geeky character, a bookworm who spent most of his times with his head buried in schoolwork- he even looked like a geek being unnaturally tall for his age and as skinny and lanky as a streak of piss. He also wore these glasses, brown rimmed national health things that looked enormous on his thin face. He didn't really fit in all that much, but he didn't mind too much either, he was quite happy being a little different. At primary school that didn't really matter much, loads of kids that age acted a little weird and there was no bullying or picking on each other as such. Also, everyone knew me and Eck had this bond despite being different and that if you messed with him, you messed with me. At secondary school we really started moving in different circles altogether, we would be moving in the same direction but we were going down different roads fairly quickly. While at primary we were always in the same classes, we were more or less split at secondary and our differences became more defined. I was mostly in the middle to bottom sets for my subjects, I wasn't remedial or anything but I did struggle with interest and motivation- I was a lazy bastard really. In truth I couldn't wait to leave to follow my dad into the factories and make some money of my own and that's what my parents saw for me and was the direction they wanted us to go down, especially dad. Thinking back, they didn't have enough money to send the two of us through education so they chose Eck or Alexander as mum always called him and that kind of suited me – I think. At breaks and lunch times I'd play pitch and toss with the lads who smoked nippers behind the bike sheds in the playground where all the people who thought they were mad used to hang out. Eck wouldn't be seen dead down there and might well have been dead if he'd dared to try. I'd use loose change and coppers to play pitchy or cards and most of the time I'd lose my lunch money and survive the day on an apple that mum had given us 'to keep the doctor away' and the glass of milk we'd get at break time. Mum used to joke that I 'only went to school for the milk' so on the days I won a few pence at pitchy I'd chuck the apple in the bin and not feel quite so guilty about wasting her money.

But football was the main thing for me at school, we'd chuck our school jumpers down for goals and playing about 26 a side in the playground or 6th years versus the school, scuffing our brand new Clarks' shoes or tearing holes in the knees of our trousers. Eck never joined in so he was spared the wrath of the mother for wrecking the school gear, while I'd get regular clips around the ear and have to suffer the embarrassment of turning up at school with brown leather patches on the elbows of my school jumpers, which was more of a punishment than the ear bashing. In class I was quite quiet and surly with the teachers. ' Are you sure you are Alex Pace's twin brother?' some would ask and say something about 'loins', which I thought was a kitchen cloth and, come to think of it, I still do. But I wasn't a bad lad and largely avoided too much trouble and rarely got the belt, other than the times I was caught smoking nippers behind the bike shed or when me and group of lads were caught giggling for opening our eyes for the duration of the Lord's Prayer at second year assembly. That was like a cardinal sin at that time, you were made to think that God would strike you down for it, but I actually think that even the teachers felt bad giving us the belt for it. I had loads of mates, normal guys, some a bit troublesome but good hearted really. I never enjoyed the work side of school but I did like the laugh with the boys and the chasing of the girls, especially later on in my school life when puberty wreaked havoc with my hormones.

Alexander was so different though, it was unbelievable to most people that we were brothers, never mind twins. At lunch times he'd be in the chess club, the library group or the book club, either that or he would be sitting in a corner of the playground studying for tests or doing his homework. We were like two very different peas from the same pod. Looking back I suppose Eck was a bit of a loner and I maybe should've made more effort at school to include him in things I did and with people I was mates with, but he didn't want to it was as simple as that. But he did have one real mate- Darren Stryde was this boy's name. Everything about them was compatible, even their names- Pace and Stryde was like a standing joke around the school. To look at them and to see the way that they hung around together, anyone who didn't know better would've assumed that they were the twin brothers rather than Eck and I. Darren Stryde was a geeky character too, to imagine him just think of your average wimpy kid and you'll have an accurate image, but for some reason I always thought there was a more sinister side to him- something I couldn't put my finger on, but it nagged away at me all the time. While Eck was more than a wee bit wet behind the ears, Darren was a wee bit more streetwise, certainly more than he would be happy to let on- I think he deliberately hid his light a bit for whatever reason. He was heavily in to drama and English Literature, particularly Oscar Wilde plays, the romantic poets and the work of the Bronte sisters. He used to go come around to our house to hang out with Eck and end up getting him to quiz him on Oscar Wilde quotes- I just thought he was weird. Eck was more mathematical and scientifically minded, he always thought things through fully and practically.

As I say, I always had this deep down irritating feeling that Darren wasn't as green as he would have you believe  and I just felt that he used Eck a wee bit, that he was the leader and Eck would dance to his every tune. I daren't mention that to Eck though, without Darren he'd have basically have been on his own and I didn't want that either and, in any case, they were as thick as thieves and didn't need me to butt in on their friendship. I felt Eck was just a bit naïve when it came to their friendship and I always thought that would come back to bite him in the arse, though I could have no idea how severe that bite would be.

I basically left school with a few low grade 'O' levels in the easiest subjects and a handful of useless modules in wood work, metal work and techy drawing. I wasn't a dunce by any means but I certainly wasn't a high flyer and school served its purpose for me- the most important thing for me to take away from it was not a piece of paper to be framed on the kitchen wall but to have gained a grounding, have a bit of manners instilled in me and generally kept me on the straight and narrow. I was glad to leave in the end and dad had set me up with a summer job sweeping the floors and being the general dogs' body in the National Cash Register factory in the town with a view to securing something more rewarding and more permanent. I loved the summer job, the banter the older lads had with me, the slagging they'd give me, the fact that they would say it straight and give me a hard boot up the arse if I left a speck of dust on the floor or two sugars in their cups of tea instead of one. I felt right at home there, much more so than I ever did at the school and I didn't even need my D at 'O' Level English to do it and still have a bit of money in my pocket.

Eck was different though, he put pressure on himself for grades and mum was overbearing in making sure that he reached his potential. She pushed and cajoled and pushed and cajoled him and pushed and cajoled him. Every single evening she would check his homework was done properly and to a very good standard. Mum would be constantly in his ear to improve it and be on his case if he ever did anything wrong. She would spend hours giving him extra tutorials in the kitchen while dad and I gave them space by playing football in the yard or tending to some household and DIY chores. I often thought the pressure was too much for Eck and mum never helped him, she just made it worse. He became very confined, insular and worried building up to his final exams and there was many a time when I would actually hear him being physically sick in the toilet in the morning of an exam. He was such a worrier as a boy and still is today. But, all told, it worked and he was a total high flyer and he got straight A's in everything. So did Darren Stryde. I was absolutely delighted for Eck, even if I would never have properly said it at the time, not with any feeling anyway, that just wasn't me.

The exam grades meant that they both enrolled in Dundee University's Law School. Eck had achieved the lifelong ambition mum had set him and, overall, he seemed really happy to have pleased her and pleased himself at the same time. He always put mum's feelings first, often to a fault. Sadly Dad died shortly after seeing Eck start Uni- they got on well despite their differences and I know that Dad was immensely proud of him and he would've loved to have seen him through Uni and helped financially. I remember spotting him dabbing a tear from his eye after watching Eck open the brown envelope containing his exam scores, ' That's my boy,' he said and slapped him hard on the back. The two of them were never particularly close and though dad's death affected him for a while, it totally knocked me for six. I couldn't accept that my father had been taken from me so suddenly, a heart attack which came without warning. Mum reacted with a stiff upper lip, she always did, but Eck was really there for me, supported me, comforted me, was a real brother to me and I never forgot that when he needed me in the future. I've been due him that debt.

Eck and Darren continued to be great mates throughout university where the gags about their surnames gathered speed (if you pardon the pun)- ' Pace and Stryde are never too far apart' being one of the most overused, but pretty funny nonetheless. But as their years of study progressed they started to come out of themselves in terms of personality, become a wee bit less geeky I suppose. They even started hanging out and chatting to members of the opposite sex, which had been an alien concept to them at school. Wednesday night was the Law society's night out in the student union and this opened up the chance for Eck to get closer to girls on the course and it was during one of these nights that he met Mary. The very same Mary Farrelly whose name you mentioned outside the church. You won't do that again that's for sure!

I reluctantly went along to a couple of those nights they had in the union. I felt like a fish out of water, but I had started working on the factory floor in the NCR and had money to spend and I got the feeling that Eck was proud of the fact that he had gathered a group of mates and wanted me to get to know them a little. I also think he wanted me to buy pints for him with my money, the poor, miserable student that he was! Straight away I could tell that this Mary lassie was a source of infatuation for Eck- he has always played his cards close to his chest and liked to give little or nothing away, but she was his Achilles heel. I would see him staring longingly over the table at her and hanging off of every word that she uttered. He would nod in agreement to anything that she said- even if I knew he blatantly disagreed with what she was saying and shook his ahead if he thought

59

that was the reaction she was seeking. To be honest, I could see why he liked her, she was fairly attractive to look at and she had a good, sparky personality- she was well able to make people laugh when she was on form. Physically they were pretty well matched, she was tall and thin like he is, but she had a shock of curly red hair ( I called it ginger, Eck said it was auburn and Mary reckoned it was a strawberry blonde. It was ginger, believe me) and pale skin with pink cheeks. Ten minutes in the sun would give the lassie sun stroke she was that pale. I have to say, though, I found her quite funny and bright and I was pleased that she seemed to take a genuine interest in Eck. You wouldn't necessarily have put the two of them together, but the idea of it wasn't too ridiculous and there were many things about them that they seemed to have in common. I could tell that she loved his intelligence; he was as sharp as a tack and was so well read that he had an almost encyclopedic knowledge about nearly every topic- apart from sport, which was about the only thing I knew anything about!

Crucially though, I could also tell that Darren was jealous of their friendship- I wasn't sure if it was because he liked Mary too or because he felt that her presence was a scourge on their friendship, but he didn't like it either way. I'd clock the way he looked on enviously when Eck and Mary were chatting and was too often quick to put Eck down or ridicule things he said in front of her. I am sure that Mary and Eck were oblivious to this, if they weren't they put up a good show of pretending. In any case it didn't bother them either way because they started going out properly at some point during their final year at Dundee Uni. Darren took really badly to it, but in fairness to him, he tried to hide his jealously from them, which he generally managed. While Darren and Eck remained best of friends on the surface at least and certainly in Eck's head, his relationship with Mary went from strength to strength and Darren slowly, but reluctantly came around to the idea that he might be sidelined every now and again in favour of the fairer sex. My mum genuinely approved of Mary too, which was of vital importance to Eck- there was always little or nothing he would do unless he was given our mother's big stamp of approval and Mary ticked all the boxes: she was good looking, bright, intelligent and, most of all, had the potential to be her own woman- a successful, professional woman, basically everything our mum had wanted to be herself, but had given up on.

Graduation day was a proud moment for my brother, although he took it largely in his stride as he did with most things by that time. His relationship with Mary was budding and it brought a bit of extra confidence out in him, he was a little more open, a bit less of a worrier. Mum, though, was beside herself with nerves and excitement; graduation day was the ultimate realisation of her ambitions for her Alexander, the perfect proof that the countless hours of hard graft that she sacrificed for her favourite son was all worthwhile. I accompanied mum to the ceremony wearing a creased, ill-fitting shirt and black kipper tie that she had bought me especially for the occasion, while she had an expensive dress and matching hand bag on for her big day. If she was preparing for her son to marry the queen she couldn't have made any more effort to look the part. I felt incredibly proud of Eck that day, he'd worked unbelievably hard for it and I really respected and loved him for that. Some people, mates of mine especially, thought I must've been jealous to see him do so well and have all the brains while I was a lowly machine factory worker, but nothing could be further from the truth. I could see that he was growing into a man and that sort of geeky image he used to have was just about gone, though he could never completely shake it off no matter how hard he tried- 'once a geek, always a geek' I would say to him! He had grown into a tall, handsome man and lost much of the gawkiness that had accompanied him through school and he definitely looked the part in his black gown and that silly mortis hat that they wear. I can still see the picture mum used to have of that day on her fire place, with Eck standing on one side grinning from ear to ear with his graduation scroll held above his head like the world cup, Darren on the other side doing the same and Mary in the middle of them with her hands around both of their waists. I still think back to that picture now, it represents something- that I know. I can even see the look in Darren's eye, that sinister side I could see of him all the way back to his school days, it's not something that the untrained eye would spot immediately, nothing starkly obvious but I knew the boy since we were bairns and there was something I found not to trust about him.

Anyway, as his relationship with Mary continued to prosper, so did his professional life. After specialising in criminal law, he worked the courts for a few years learning his trade and getting used to defending some of the city's low lives. I thought he'd be more suited to business or property law than the defence stuff- I just though him too morally upstanding to defend some of the arseholes he knew were guilty, but that was his choice – and Darren's too. Darren was ruthlessly ambitious and always had an eye for making money and once they had the experience under their belts he and Eck set up a business of their own defending the great and the good of Dundee's underworld. Stryde & Pace 'One Step Ahead of the Law' was what they called it and it succeeded in attracting all the petty thieves, junkies and house burglars you could ever have the displeasure of seeing. You know them, the kind of people you see hanging about outside the front of the Wellgate Centre of a Friday evening. They built a reputation as a couple of young, well turned out high fliers who had a knack of finding loopholes in the law and the silver tongued, persuasive powers to encourage less severe punishments for convicts. It was a murky job and not one that I though suited my brother very much- it was definitely more Ecky than Alexander- but they were successful enough to make a good rake of money and Eck bought himself a nice house on the Perth Road, which he shared with Mary when they married which was always going to be the natural route their relationship would take. Darren and I were his two best men, but even then I could tell Darren was still jealous, he had never held onto a girlfriend of his own and I think he was frustrated to see his best mate so happy.

After graduating Mary didn't specialise and started working in Stryde & Pace 'One Step Ahead of the Law' in more or less an administrative role, which to me was another way of saying she was the secretary. I thought she lacked ambition despite the fact that she had an eye for the finer things in life. Eck, though, insisted that she put in the hours and worked extremely hard, often staying behind for hours long after the lawyers had gone home to deal with paperwork, sometimes not getting home until 8 or 9 o'clock in the evening. I remember around a year after they married me and my fiancé Angela would go out with them in the town on a Saturday night for a meal or a couple of pints. The four of us got on well enough, although we would otherwise move in totally different circles. Angela would tell me that she thought Mary was too often harsh with Eck, sometimes cheeky and aloof and would regularly speak down to him. Angela thought he deserved to be treated with more respect than his wife was showing him. I must say, I am pretty perceptive and I never really noticed anything particularly untoward, and I'd be sensitive to people getting at Eck all our lives, but I thought it was nothing more significant than a typical man and wife who'd bicker a little bit. She would tell me that it was woman's intuition, I would pretend to agree.

Darren, meanwhile, continued to be hard-nosed with ambition, much more so than Eck, and this led to some cracks in their business relationship and, as a result, their friendship. Darren would literally take on any client, regardless of his feelings about the crimes they'd committed or his gut instinct about their guilt, to ensure money flowed into the business. Eck would be more picky about who he'd defend and believed that their reputation as lawyers would be dragged through the mud if they were not more selective. I could see a distance growing between him and Eck as a result of this- Darren would complain that Eck was turning business down, but he'd just shrug his shoulders and say something about 'morals before money' that would piss Darren off even more. Eck was just more laid back about the business than his partner was and this was a source of conflict. It would be an exaggeration to say that I could see their relationship breaking down, but I certainly had a bit of an inkling that everything wasn't as Eck would've liked it to be, or even thought it was. Sometimes Eck is not the best judge of character, he's naïve to a fault. I think that because he's had so few real friends in his life he sees the best in everyone and I think that ended up being his downfall in terms of the relationships with people that he'd assumed were closest to him.

Mainly due to Darren's bloody, bloody mindedness and desire to catch more than just the early worm, business was at worst brisk and, at times, heaving. This led to Mary spending more and more time going down to the office, generally dealing with Darren's paper work and what he called 'overspill.' Eck wasn't even remotely suspicious about the amount of time Mary was spending at the office after normal hours, it wasn't his way. He was an honest soul, a guy who saw the best in everyone, particularly those who he assumed had earned his trust. Eck thought that Mary was simply working hard, putting in the hours, showing the type of commitment to her job that he admired, an attitude he had spotted the first time they met in tutorials and grew to love unconditionally. Little did he know, the conditions were not his to make. Indeed, they'd been made for him.

I can recall the night it all came out like it was yesterday. Eck was growing anxious, which was really unlike him. It was late, very late, beyond 11 bells if I remember rightly and, although Mary had been in the habit of burning the midnight oil in the office to help with Darren's large bundle of paper work, she'd never been this long, not without contacting home at least. Eck's was pacing around his living room, twitching the curtains and each minute that passed without the sound of Mary's heels crunching up the driveway increased his worry. He tried to call the office several times, only for it to ring out. His worry increased with every unanswered ring. That was it, though, it was worry, fear for her safety- a woman alone in an office late at night or a woman making her way home in the dark on a cold winter's evening or a woman who could encounter trouble or danger at the turn of a city centre street.

Also, my brother's fears were irrationally increased given the line of work that they were in. Stryde & Pace 'One Step Ahead of the Law' had been targeted before, all sorts of 'small town crims' as they'd call them on the box, had been through those doors. Court verdicts would be held against the lawyers who tried to defend the often indefensible. Even not guilty verdicts caused problems through disgruntled victims baying for blood. What if one of these cases had come back to haunt them? What if she'd been mugged? Or perhaps kidnapped? Even raped? The worst thoughts ran through Eck's head like a burst dam.

Eventually he decided to head down to the office himself. Inside he had that feeling, that sixth sense that something was truly wrong. That gut churning nag that what was going to meet him when he arrived was going to reluctantly agree with his primordial fears. He opened the door to the office and was met with silence. He called his wife's name and there was no response. He walked through to her office and there it was in front of him. The moment that would alter his life forever.....

Alan had barely touched his pint, save the large gulp he consumed as George started his tale. George cocked his head and pursed his lips downwards as he stroked the outside of his tumbler with his thick thumb and forefingers.

' Tak yir time George,' Alan interjected, ' Eh can kinda guess what happened next. Yi dinnae need tae go on, it'll only upset you,' he said clutching George's arm.

George nodded slowly. ' It's ok Al. Eh'll tell yi the rest. It's just a wee bit tough ken what I mean? Eh never, ever speak aboot this. It's been a banned subject for decades. But it's been the elephant in the room for what seems like forever. It changed all of our lives. Ruined Eck's and in turn ruined mine too. Eh think it will dae me the power o' good to talk about it tae be honest,' he added somberly.

' Well only if yir sure,' Alan said sympathetically. ' Listen, eh'll get yi another pint and myself a wee chaser and yi can tell us the rest. I'm all ears and you seem thirsty....' Alan said without waiting for a response as he limped to the bar.

George stared into the middle distance and ran through the rest of that fateful night in mind. Shaking his head ruefully his mind shifted to his twin brother: ' Poor fuckin' bugger, eh hope that he's ok,' he whispered                              to                              himself

# 10

## INSOMNIA

The mist lingers threateningly above the faded silvery waters of the River Tay as a faint opening in the curtains invites in a modicum of gloomy light as the bruised purple sky starts to heal over. The neon digital alarm flashes at 5.28am as the colon indicating each passing second of their lives pulses with monotony towards sunrise.

At either side of the room the brothers lie awake. They are secretly aware of each other's insomnia. George lies facing the bare wall that stands lazily just a foot in front of his nose. His head accepts the therapeutic invitation from the off white pillow as he nurses the effects of staying out long into the evening with Alan. Through a fuzzy head, he reflects internally on Alexander's reaction to Alan and his mentioning of Mary Farrelly's name. Had he let his brother down by staying out later than expected? After all, he knew he was upset and would've been looking for a shoulder to cry on- his shoulder. Had he let his brother down by breaking his confidence, telling his story?

George's nauseating feelings of guilt were intertwined with pangs of relief from sharing his past with a sympathetic ear. It felt liberating. And how he enjoyed a day of relative freedom away from Alexander's burdening woes. 'Was that bad?' he thought to himself. Life should be more like last night, he thinks to himself. He wants more of it- a natter, a pint with old friends, sharing things in common, trading experiences and life stories, catching up on old times and memories, not stuck here in this dreary prison cell with my two shadows for 'company', not to mention those patronising nurses who treat me like I'm an old age fuckin' bairn.

Alexander stares at the ceiling, his eyes squinting for light, he silently seethes. Questions swirl around his head like an impending tsunami, callously swarming his troubled mind, his bed frame squeaking as he shuffles around seeking a position of temporary mental calmness. Instead his mind is befuddled with questions of regret which open up in his mind in ever increasing circles. Why did George not come back early when he knew I was so distressed? How could he treat me like that? Why did that friend of his have to mention that woman's name to me? How does he know her? How did he know we were a couple? Why on earth do I care? But I do. I really, really do not want to but I do. I really do.

' George, are you awake? ' Alexander whispers loudly, puncturing the perfect peace provided by the pitch dark of the night. His calling is met with eerie silence, his words tumbling off in time never to be answered. He gives it a few seconds, less than ten but more than five, his patience on a short leash:

' George ….. George …….., George……. Ahem,' he coughs exaggeratedly. ' George…. Eh George… GEORGE! GEORGE PACE!! Are you awake? Can you hear me? I know full well that you are awake. I really need to speak with you George. Are you listening to me George? ' Alexander repeats his whisper, upping the ante with the volume and vociferousness of its delivery. But the deafeningly silent response is repeated with the addition of a faux groaning sound emanating from beneath the duvet on the other side of the room.

George is awake, wide awake other than a fuzzy haze from last night's alcohol intake that slightly hinders his clarity of thought. Alexander knows his brother's awake, he watched him as he stumbled in at 12.26am last night, this morning even, his walking stick clanging off the bed post and radiator, his motor control skills betraying his attempts to arrive unnoticed like a tipsy teenager trying to sneak upstairs past his mammy's bedroom with a mouthful of extra strong mints. Now George pretends to sleep, facing the wall with eyes wide shut, grabbing the chance of some extra minutes' peace before facing the straining notes of his angry brother's music.

' George.........., George........., George ............., George...... Psssst, GEORGE JOHN PACE! Ach, listen, I know full well that you are awake. Listen, I am not angry with you, I am just disappointed that you didn't come back earlier. You knew I was upset and needed you last night. You could have at least come back earlier, you didn't need to stay out all night. I mean you didn't even want to go to the funeral in the first place. Or so you said at least.' Alexander's whisper has become more of an audible carp. He knows George is awake, George knows he knows he is awake, but temporary ignorance is temporary bliss. He'll deal with it when morning proper comes. In any case, he thinks to himself, as if he's not been there for his brother enough times. It's not his fault that the man is an emotional wreck, the mere mention of a name sending him into a tailspin again. In fact, he thinks to himself, he couldn't have done more to help him recover from the woe that women caused him over the years, how dare he get fucking angry with me for escaping this fucking claustrophobia hell for a measly few hours. He is tempted to respond, to rouse himself out of his fake slumber and bite at the dangling bait, but he opts to sleep on it, hold his tongue, bite his lip, swallow an enormous gulp of his fury. Or pretend to at least.

Alexander exhales a sigh of lamentation which echoes through the dawning night air and gives up his cajoling for the minute, opting to tussle with his thoughts for a while longer. He averts his gaze back from his slumbering sibling to a spot on the ceiling that holds his glare. Troubled thoughts tumble from his mind to the roof. He has spent years batting away memories of the past, swatting them away like a flee ridden dog. But the more he tries to bat them off, the harder and more venomous they come back like a plague of limpets feasting on their vulnerable prey.

He spent yesterday evening convalescing with Nurse Mabel on his return from Jimmy Brown's funeral in an attempt to recover from the shock that reverberated through him in the grounds of Downfield South Church. The very mention of that woman's name shook his inner being to the core and the lonely drive back to the Riverview Nursing and Retirement Home passed unconsciously with a numbed blur, a fuzzy haze of rebounding abhorrent memories he's tried so hard to consign to the dust bin.

Nurse Mabel greeted him instantly on his return, he'd engineered his walk through the communal area perfectly to accidently on purpose collide with her at work on her duties. ' Why are you back so early Alexander? Where is George? Is he not with you? My, you look as pale as a ghost, have a seat here and I'll fetch you a drink,' she said indulging Alexander's unsaid demand for a sympathetic ear. Nurse Mabel dutifully puffed up a cushion and, with an open palm and smile of concern, she invited Alexander to sit back on a high backed red leather chair and fetched him a soothing cup of hot chocolate.

' Oh thank you so much Nurse Mabel, I feel as weak as a straw. I most probably would have collapsed if you hadn't been here when I arrived in. I really have come over a little poorly I'm concerned to say,' Alexander said attaching his trembling left hand symbolically to centre of his chest and inhaling exaggeratedly as his right hand clutched the small of his back.

Nurse Mabel is wise enough to take Alexander's physical complaints with a chubby handed fist full of salt, but could tell that his appearance was ashen enough to indicate some kind of shock. ' Oh, what's wrong Alexander?' she said, placing her hand concernedly just above the knee of Alexander's spindly left leg, an action that encouraged a slight shiver to move through his skeletal bones. ' Is there something you want to talk about? Something you need to say to someone? I mean, where is George? This is the first time I have ever seen the two of you apart since you came here,' Nurse Mabel continued in a tone that soothed Alexander's concerns just a little and encouraged a little openness from a naturally closed book. There was something about the attention of a woman, a woman in a position of authority in particular, that encouraged Alexander to let down his guard slightly. He feels genuinely comfortable in the company of Nurse Mabel, the warm feeling of cotton wool protection that the closeness to a woman brings him, a feeling that he's been devoid of for too many decades, never mind days, weeks or even years.

Nurse Mabel listened intently with an indulgent ear, shuffling close enough for her knees to graze off of his, as Alexander inched his cards from their regulation position packed vice like against his chest. By nature he covets his own thoughts, preferring them to spiral turbulently around in his own head rather than pestering the mind of others. George has long been his confidante, but he opened up slightly to Nurse Mabel, but only slightly. His story was told with seismic gaps

He told Nurse Mabel that a friend of George's had said something to him outside the church, but neglected to mention that that something was the name of his ex-wife, the very woman whom he had loved with all his being and had dedicated his life and heart to. He told Nurse Mabel that what was said had upset him desperately, but neglected to add that the mere mention of that name- Mary Farrelly, Mary Pace had swung him irreversibly. He told Nurse Mabel that George had known that what his friend had said outside the church had upset him and that he was disappointed in him for not coming back earlier to check on his welfare, but neglected to mention that it was George Pace, his often surly but ever faithful sibling, who had been there to extricate him from his lowest ebb, to single handily drag him back from the brink of self-destruction to the detriment of his own personal contentment.

' Deary me, that sounds like an awfully bad night for you Alexander. What that person said must have been really bad to upset you so much,' Nurse Mabel had said, hopeful that her genuine curiosity might encourage Alexander to reveal all.

' Oh, it was awful Nurse Mabel, but if you don't mind I'd rather not talk about it for now. I've only just recovered from the shock, but thanks for listening to me bleating on, I'm sure you have better things to be doing than listening to some of my woes,' Alexander replied, moving the cards back nearer his chest.

' Ach, don't be silly Alexander,' Nurse Mabel said in that thinly masked patronising tone that George finds so offensive but his brother loves so much, ' Sure, that's what I am here for, I wouldn't be doing my job right for you otherwise. Now would you like a cup of something hot and I'll help you off to your room.'

' That would be great Nurse Mabel, maybe a hot chocolate would help me sleep,' Alexander said clutching various parts of his body as he rises from the chair to his feet, ' I really do wish George would hurry home though, what keeps him this late?' he says glancing down at his watch.

' I'm sure he'll be back soon Alexander, now don't you go worrying about that.'

Nurse Mable linked arms with Alexander, helping him with his faux shuffle along the dank corridor towards the room he now calls home. Each step is met with a groan or a moan or a yelp or a gasp. Opening the door she offered Alexander into his room, he accepted.

' Age before beauty,' he said with the hint of a wink.

Nurse Mabel smiled and reached up to give him a conciliatory pat him on the shoulder, ' Shit before the shovel don't you mean?' she jokes. Alexander reciprocates with a stifled nod. 'Now relax there and I'll fetch your hot chocolate.'

With that the door closed on him, leaving him alone with his thoughts. An audience with the devil and his daughter. Surveying the room's bare walls and garish décor Alexander feels strangely safe and at home with its lack of outside influences, its insular feeling, its lack of the threats of the outside world that he hid away from for so long. Out with the gaze of his brother, he strides across to the blackening window above his bed, he thwacks back the curtains, and looks both ways along the street before slumping down on pale yellow bedding that covers his bed, ' I wish you'd hurry home George. I wish you'd hurry home my brother.'

# 11

## ICE COLD

' Now listen right here the noo ya silly cunt and do not feed me any mare o' yir shite ,' George barks angrily having ultimately succumbed to his brother's incessant attempts to rouse him. Mimicking a snooty accent he rasps, ' The last thing that you said to me was 'you stay and have a pint, I'm going home, I feel all weak at the knees. All the usual shite that eh should not have tae put up wi. No, honestly, you said, 'you stay for as long as you please. ' And noo yi have the fuckin' cheek tae moan because I had a few fuckin' drinks with an auld pal fae the fitba! I'll tell yi Eck, you're like a fuckin' ball and chain, yir worse than any fuckin' woman e've ever met in meh life. Now gee me some peace. Eh need tae sleep.'

Deliberately placing his left hand on his chest and marrying it with a well versed open mouthed gasp, Alexander briefly, deliberately, acts agog, dumbstruck by the intensity and force of his sibling's ire. He can tell that, this time, George's fury is for real, no pet anger for the sake of vent. The 'c' word is a dead giveaway: 'If yi ever do hear me say any four letter word beggin' with c then yi ken em awa tae bang somebody's puss,' thinks Alexander, his mind briefly zoned out to bygone conversations. He knows well that George can blow off steam by turning the air blue on occasion, but he also is well practised in spotting when the blurred line into fury has been battered down. And Alexander is clear, this is no brother to be crossed with when in this humour, or lack of.

You see, Alexander had assumed on a life where his past remained a figment, a series of embarrassing stills and frames confined to the annals and never to see the light of day again. But the dusty, murky recesses were temporarily wiped away last night, however briefly, and what lurked underneath made unpleasant viewing. The outlandish elephant in the darkroom's name was uttered. 'How dare he mention her name in my company,' Alexander had said over and over as he tossed and turned on his pillow last night. It was a rare fit of pique in a life that he had slowly, slowly, slowly turned into a tranquil denial. Perched on the end of his bed, Alexander's mind turns to that fateful night. The barriers he has placed up to filter any thoughts about it have prevented him ever allowing it to enter his consciousness. But deep down, he can never forget it. How could he? It has shaped his mind set, changed his life and the life of the brother he covets and loves despite appearances.

Deep in his soul he remembers slowly turning the key with a black gloved hand at the front door of the offices of Stryde & Pace 'One Step Ahead of the Law'. It was a large red coloured door which opened onto the street. As it creaked awake, it invited an icy blast up the concrete stairwell, a single newspaper page ignorantly forcing its way ahead of him in the stiffening late November breeze. The stairwell was dank and damp and captured the whining breeze as Alexander climbed the steps, each stride mirroring his thumping heart which battered against his rib cage like a clothed mallet. Exhaling loudly, he held onto the paint pealed hand rail, his glove inadvertently rubbing the invisible finger prints of some of the city's most notorious felons free.

Alexander fumbled in his jacket pocket for the keys to the inside door, his hands trembling as he removed his leather gloves and inserted the faded gold key into the rusting lock. He pulled the door slightly towards himself them pushed it open with his whip thin shoulder. The offices were pitched mainly in winter darkness save an amber lighting emanating from the crack at the foot of his wife's office door. Alexander stood poker straight, only the movement of his frosted breath provided movement as it filled the stairwell with increasing regularity.

' Mary……. Mary…. Mary…. Mary! Are you in there?' he called, each holler increasing in its volume and stress. His mind was working in slow motion as the nerves wreaked havoc with his clarity of thought. His mind considered what might await him behind his wife's office door. No response was forthcoming. He had hoped for anything, even a muffled grunt. Any sign of life. Alexander thought of the waifs, strays, small time crooks and much, much worse who'd been defended in this building, how morals and gut instincts had played second fiddle to business and the making of a living. Societies' lowest rung had used this place as a crutch and many had their liberty rescinded- but many others must have held grudges despite their heinous guilt. Who knows who could've sought retribution…

Alexander creaked the door open and peered into Mary's office as it lay ajar. Opening it full, a light from a single lamp illuminated the oak wooden table, which Alexander instinctively noted was tidier than normal. The nature of his job had made his attention to small details razor sharp. At the centre of the table sat a white envelope, brightened by the light and waiting like a beacon in his glare.

With cautious haste, Alexander shifted his gangly frame. From close by he could tell that it was a letter intended for him, his name scrawled on the front in black biro pen. Tearing the seal, he removed the note and immediately scrambled to the end to see who it was from. Mary. Then to the top. He scanned the letter disbelievingly then read every word deliberately one by one they represented a knife to his heart:

Dear Alexander,

This has been the most difficult decision of my life, please believe me when you read these words. There was no easy way of saying this so I have written it in this letter. To have told you face to face would have been too tough and I could not bear to see you upset. I know it is a coward's way out but I couldn't do it any other way. Tonight I am leaving you. I no longer love you though I do admire and respect you, I can no longer live with you. I have been feeling this way for some time but have regretfully neglected to communicate these feelings to you. I did love you and that was the case for most of our time together but those feelings have gone now. Please believe me when I say that I have tried to get those feelings for you back. When we made love last week I felt nothing, no passion or desire and it was then that I knew our time was over. I tried to win back that spark but it was gone.

Now this is the part that will really hurt you and please believe me when I have tried to stop this happening, I have fallen in love with Darren and he has fallen in love with me. It has not been long term but the feelings have been growing and we have decided to leave the city together to set off on another life. He feels as bad as I do because he is your best friend and he never intended to let you down in this way, but we both feel the same. Please believe us when we say that this is not a decision we have taken lightly and has not been done on a whim. Darren intends that the business will be left with you entirely, though this is for another day I'm sure.

By the time you have read this letter, Darren and I will have left. I packed a small bag before I left home and you can set fire to or dump the rest of my belongings if you want. I have to move on and cannot come back. Believe me when I say that I am so, so, so sorry that I have done this to you, but there was no other way. My lawyers will be in touch to start the proceedings for our divorce. I will not be demanding anything from you.

Have a good life because you deserve much, much better than this and much better than me.

Love always,

Mary.

The icy coldness of those words chilled Alexander's bones. A quivering shiver ran raggedly to every extremity of his being. Speechless, his moist eyes fixated on the page, anger almost burning a hole through his spouse's name. Love always? The effing bitch. How dare she write that? Love always? Strangely, he felt no pity for himself, time would bring that, he did not feel upset or sad or morose or a sense of loss or longing or a desire to reverse time. He was simply consumed by the most overpowering feeling of fury, a feeling so alien to him he felt like he was suffering an out of body experience. It felt like a dream, the wildest, most bizarre nightmare imaginable but one he would never wake up from. He remembers that night they made love, he felt nothing different yet all along she was wanting to be with his friend, his so called kindred spirit, the inseparable Pace and Stryde now driven apart through whimsical human desires. Alexander felt nothing for Darren Stryde, he would never waste a second of his life concerned about him. From that moment his name and the picture he had of him in his head was airbrushed from his memory bank. George had warned him to be wary and had long suggested that there was a sinister edge to Darren, but Alexander had never seen it and batted these suggestions away out of hand. Deep down though he had always known that Darren was envious of his relationship with Mary, he saw her as someone who could come between their friendship and the closeness of their bond, but not for a nanosecond had he considered that this jealously would manifest itself in the ultimate betrayal. But Darren's betrayal was not of chief concern. Friends can come and go, even your best ones, even your business partner that you've spent the majority of your life looking out for and sharing the bad times and the good. But more salient in his thoughts was how Mary could do this to him. How could she possibly betray him like this after all they had been through and all that he had done for her?

With those handwritten words on that letter, a curtain was drawn on his life. Since then he has prepared for his decline. Only the ultimate fate will ever bring him clarity and confidence.

## 12

## AWAY DAY

The two following days acted like a sticking plaster to heal the brothers' rift. Alexander knew well to steer clear of his seething brother, confortable in the notion that his steam would ultimately blow out and that the bite would not follow the bark. Similarly, Alexander needed head space of his own. Alan Patterson's words had opened a sore and the years of whitewashing any thoughts of his marital woes and the stunning loss of his wife and best friend in one fail swoop. The head space had allowed Alexander to compartmentalize his thought processes and relegate those ill feelings to the darker crannies of his mind. Alexander also knew it was in his wisest interests not to push the funeral outings and had taken to secretly perusing his updates on rip.co.uk from out with his seething sibling's scowling eyeshot.

This didn't stop him feeling that this hiatus meant that he was missing out on the mourning. The e-mail updates told him that Edgar Moller had passed away peacefully at 95, 'an inspirational teacher and friend to many.' He had taught Alexander Higher Maths at Dundee's Harris Academy and was one of few people who could make calculus, trigonometry and the theorem of Pythagoras even remotely interesting. That, Alexander believes, more than warrants his presence at the funeral. Maurice Davis had also departed at 91, 'a wise local councilor very much loved by his family.' Davis had worked in the West End constituency for many a long year, impressing Alexander with his work, even though he had never spoken to him in his life. Alexander sent messages of condolence for both dead men's families over the World Wide Web, blissfully aware that neither family would have even the slightest notion as to who Mr. Alexander Pace is. For now, the mourning would have to wait, there were rifts to be healed.

Today's breakfast is a Saturday treat in The Riverview Nursing and Retirement Home. The perfectly poached eggs , smoked salmon and toasted homemade brown bread was consumed in relative peace, save a few incredulous grunts from George punctuating the clanging of silver cutlery, scraping of butter and sibilant sipping of tea.

Following several inanities, Alexander broke through another period of uncomfortable silence. ' So what are you planning for today George? It's another lovely looking day you know. You know what I might do, and you are more than welcome to join me, I might have a trip to Broughty Ferry and take a stroll along the beach front. Do you fancy that at all? We could even go for an ice cream at that Italian place if the sun is still shining.'

' No thanks,' George replies with his head full of other ideas. 'Em actually gonna go to Dens Park today, I've no been for ages and quite fancy a wee change. Dundee are playing United, should be a good ain. Definitely mare interesting than a funeral anyway, although the form the Dees have been in recently there's nae guarantee of that. By all accounts the atmosphere at Dens these days has been mare like a morgue recently than some of the funerals you've been taking me to! At least the pehs are better though,' George added only half in myrth.

'Oh…. Oh, em ok, no bother George, you do what pleases yourself. That's not a bother at all,' Alexander replies trying desperately to cloak his disappointment as he drains the remaining remnants of his lukewarm cup of tea. ' The last time I was at Dens was when Alan Gilzean and Ian Ure were playing, that must be over 40 years ago at least. Remember dad used to take us in and lift us on his shoulders to see the matches? Them's the days eh George. You know what? I might take a trip along with you myself.'

' Oh no yi dinna! You're no comin' wee me tae the match!' George bristled, ' You dinna ken the first thing aboot fitba and you'd just embarrass me if you came. Besides dinna kid yersel on, you were never at the matches we me and dad when we were bairns. You speak aboot it like yi were the Dark Blues' biggest fan. You would normally spend Saturday afternoons shopping we yir mother!' he adds mockingly. George had loved those days as a kid, Saturday afternoons at 3 o'clock with his old man lifting him over the turnstyle, 'can we give the young lad a lifty o'er' he would say. They'd stand on the terracing, George senior lifting his son onto his shoulders to grab a peak of the action amongst the smoke filled air which was turned blue with choice football banter. It was what George junior imagined himself to be like in the future- taking his son to the match on a Saturday, sharing that raw, earthy passion with like-minded fans. Fate, however, has dealt him a more complex hand, in many ways a hand he has reluctantly accepted and played.

' No need to be so rude about it George. Well, you go on yersel as you and your football buddies say. See if I care. I've a lot to do myself anyway and all the swearing that goes on between those rowdy fans is not my cup of tea anyway. Anyway those seats that you have to sit in are no use for my back ache and the lack of leg room does nothing for my rheumatism,' Alexander replies snootily, revealing a snobbish side which is his default defensive mechanism.

' Well Eck, I'm meeting my mate Alan Patterson for a wee pint before the game in the Centenary Bar so dinna you worry about me being on meh ain. Remember Alan fae the funeral, the man you made a fool oot of me in front of?' George isn't looking at Alexander, he doesn't need to, he already knows his reaction. Hurt, upset, neglected, left out. Without making his excuses, Alexander leaves the table, tossing his crumb filled serviette on top of his half eaten toast. George watches as his brother's gangly frame ambles towards the door where he clutches his back briefly before exiting. As the door wheezes closed he feels a mixture of pity and recrimination.

Alexander has been, George believes, a shackling, all-consuming influence on him for too long. A pint with his mate and a pie and Bovril at the match may represent scant change to most, but is the type of simple pleasure that George yearns for and is regularly denied. But deep down he loves his brother and he knows well that his love is reciprocated though often played out through a needy cling. George believes that his brother has never had closure on the woes of his past, his inability to face up to the treachery of those closest to him means that it remains a gyrating gorilla on both of their backs, the elephant in the room that can never be talked about but everyone is aware of its brooding presence.

The full stop at the end of Mary's dear John letter  was symbolic, a tiny black dot that marked the closing of a chapter. But it not only brought an end to Alexander's two closest relationships it brought the termination of the spirit and soul within him. From that moment forward he clambered within himself, withdrawn and reclusive like a timid puppy. For years he locked himself away behind the closed doors of the house he once shared with his wife, answering to nobody, not even George. Letters piled up behind the door and dust grew untended on the window sill as everything slipped out of his grasp. His professional life went to rack and ruin, no attempts made to continue with **Pace and Stryde: One** Step Ahead of the Rest. From that day forward the doors closed and the company ceased business, the city's reprobates left to find alternative means of defence  in a world where, Alexander believes, the most heartless, heinous moral crimes have been committed against him.

The brothers' respective Saturday afternoon's outings reflect just about all that is needed to be known about the manifest diversity their shared nature has engendered. They are both Pace boys, but are infinitesimal yards apart in personality, interests and what makes their lives tick.

Alexander sits all brooding and reflective on a bench in the bandstand at the top of the rolling greenery of Magdalen Green, whose sloping undulations amble gently towards a daily meeting with the lusty waters of the silvery River Tay. The mouth of the meandering river has lost its silver sheen today and Alexander peers out over his spectacles to see the dull horizon exchanging pleasantries with a lingering mist that has mugged his eyes of his view of the Tay Rail Bridge. The waves lap gently against the old stone wall that separates the river from the winding Riverside Walk. The pavement hosts a fledgling couple who walk blissfully arm in arm as their yelping dog sniffs and tugs at his lead. The scene invites Alexander to internally recite the opening of Shakespeare's Sonnet number 60,

' *Let the waves make towards the pebbled shore,*

*So do our minutes hasten to their end,*

*Each changing place with that which goes before,*

*In sequant toil all forwards do contend'.*

Alexander sees each wave lap up and die out, only to be replaced by another. It is, he believes, like the seconds of his life which flicker by-one after the other, after the other, before the next. Alexander does not want his life to end, but he wants the life he has been forced to live to die out.

The bandstand, which Alexander notices needs a good lick of paint, brings with it a particular resonance. It was here that George had proposed to Angie, a proposal he had assumed would pave the way for a lifelong partnership to take on the world. Deep in the core of his being, Alexander knows that it is he who has taken that partnership out of the hands and heart of his brother and that the partnership George is left with has rendered him unfulfilled. Perhaps that is why he comes down to the bandstand in times of somber solace, a subliminal display of apologetic sorrow for his sibling. Perhaps, he considers, one day he can set his brother free. But how?

Alexander inhales deeply, rubbing the bottom of his back before removing a creased, rolled up copy of the Dundee Courier newspaper from the back pocket of his fawn coloured trousers. He turns hastily to the back, flicking through the sports pages without even the merest glance of interest and turns the paper outside in and open at the hatch, match and dispatch section. Removing a luminous yellow marker pen from his left hand pocket, he crosses his long legs and leans back against the black painted bench. ' Ok, let's see what next week has in store for George and I,' he murmurs to himself, shifting around to find a position of more comfort for his rangy limbs.

'Ok, the A's. Allison, Bernard- Peacefully after a long fight with lung cancer at the FiveWays Nursing Home at Coldside, Dundee. Beloved widow of wife Jillian and survived by three beloved children Max, Jason and Michelle. Funeral will take place at the Crematorium then afterwards in the Invercarse Hotel. All donations are welcome to the Cancer Research . Now, do I know old Bernie, let me think now......'

Meantime, in a mind set far, far away, George sits reflectively, if not somewhat pensively, in the Centenary Bar on Clepington Road, a popular pre match haunt for football fans on both sides of the Dundee divide. The hallowed turf of Dens Park and its incumbents is situated less than five minutes away and the short walk to Dens intersects between it and Dundee United' s Tannadice Park, the two closest professional football stadiums in the world. But a brooding rivalry creates a distance between the red, white and blue and the black and tangerine halves of the city. It is impossible to think that George's mind might be in any shape or form, on Alexander and his newspaper and the list of the names of people young and old who have died in his home city and its surrounding areas over the past couple of days. But somewhere, somehow, a small part of his mind just can't help the nagging sorrow he feels for his twin. He parks the thought, flicking his eyes to deny it further access to his mind. His mind drifts quickly to Angie and how she'd wait for him in the

Centenary Bar after matches with a Gin and slim tonic, watching the door to see his disposition as he walked through and judge whether it reflected victory or, as was all too often, abject misery and defeat. No matter what, though, the second he walked through the door the result seemed irrelevant, there was life beyond the score in a lousy football match and, other than for a couple of hours on a Saturday afternoon, that life revolved around the love of his soon to be wife. Secretly he bemoans the way that his life has turned out. He never had much, but then he never asked for much. He recalled that how, when Christmas time came along, his brother would write a list as long as his arm for Santa to bring him, and how he'd throw his absent toys from the pram on Christmas morning when all but one or two of his demands never arrived. George, conversely, never asked for much because he never wanted much. But what he could not have expected was that, all these decades later, he has nothing of the little he ever wanted. Again, he parked the negative thoughts into neutral. After all, he was here to enjoy himself and, back in his reality, he is in his element, removed from the sterile environs of the nursing home with its dreary wallpaper and the claustrophobic presence of his overbearing brother. Instead he drinks in the buzz of anticipation that precedes any match, particularly a season opening derby.

As he waits on his friend to arrive, George looks around and sees fans sporting the colours of both clubs mingling happily, all talking over each other, bantering inconsequently about who has the better team. George allows his mind to wander nostalgically back to the days when his father would take him down to Dens Park as a kid, how he'd dress him in his winter wollies and the team scarf and walk speedily across the park with him struggling to keep up. He remembers how he'd buy him a pie and a Bovril to warm him up and ask the old man on the turnstiles if he could, 'lift the wee lad over,' to get him in for free. He remembers a time when they arrived for a Scottish Cup quarter final against United at Tannadice, how they'd walked excitedly through the throng to reach the ground only to discover that the 'Sold Out' signs had been slapped across the turnstiles. He remembers how a woman hanging from the window of a top floor tenement house overlooking Tannadice saw him crying inconsolably and shouted over to his father, ' Do want to bring that wee lad up here to watch it? That'll stop him greetin'. You can see the pitch fae up here,' the woman hollered and up they went on an adventure he'd recount to his school buddies the next day.

George's thoughts are interrupted,' So, here he is, George Pace as eh live and breath,' Alan's thin angular frame limping its way to across to his a table carrying a pint of Guinness which appears to have the weight of a lead instrument.

' I see you've no changed much anyway, I see you got yesel one anyway,' laughs George half in joke, three quarters in earnest.

' Oh shit George, sorry eh'll get yi ain, selfish bastard eh am,' Alan says shuffling his thin hand into his pocket, pulling out a stained handkerchief as loose change made mainly out of copper falls to the wooden floor.

' Dinna be ridiculous Alan, eh've got this here, eh wis just pullin yir leg ' George nods in the direction of the lager he's been nursing since he arrived, ' In any case the match will be kicked aff beh the time you get to the bar judging by the speed you were walking across the bar at there!'

' And you're ain tae talk, your near enough a bloody cripple, you and that bloomin' walking stick that was makin' ah that flamin' noise at Broony's funeral!' Alan japes mischievously.

The two men laugh uproariously. It is an unusual sight to see George's disposition break so freely from its natural grim default. He has one of these faces that induces such sympathy when he laughs that you nearly wish he's revert back to type for fear it may bring a tear to the eye. But this is what he loves and misses, the light hearted banter, the teasing and the piss taking that it is impossible to indulge in with Alexander, such is his brother's uber sensitivity and mental scarring.

' So how's that brother oh yours after the other night George? Has he got over me mentioning that Mary Farrelly's name? I'll tell yi, eh didnae expect that response when eh mentioned her name. I always knew her as a nice lassie,' Alan inquires tentatively sipping from his Guinness and licking the frothy remnants from his upper lip.

George had rather have avoided the subject but rather than give Alan the short shrift he would prefer, he appreciates that his interests is based on concern and, deep down, that is something that pleases him.

' He's no bad, no great though ken? Just the usual eh? He'll never get over it, he is really just seeing his time oot but he cannot really handle life in the real world and that's why he's ended up in the retirement hame before he's ready, or we're ready I should say. It's comfy in there fir him, nobody tae bather him or ask him any questions. The women look efter him and he loves it that way. That's what the funerals are aboot tae eh? It's no that he indulges in other's misfortune, it's that he genuinely feels an empathy for their broken hearts and thinks that he's dayin them a favour beh turning up, even when they dinnae ken him fae Adam,' George says, his words a mixture of compassion and frustration.

' Eh, but it cannae be easy for you George, livin' in a hole like that before yir time. There's surely tae God mare fir yi tae be dayin than rolling up at Tom, Dick and Harry's funeral every day,' says Alan.

' But that's what brothers are fir Alan. Blood is thicker than water and all that. It's no just any Tam, Dick and Harry either in fairness. He does ken the Tam, Dick and Harrys whose funerals he goes tae, even if it's in his ain head,' George replies sharply, he's slightly irked. ' And is you'd have seen him efter his wife and best mate did the dirty on him, you would understand how he has needed me there fir him.

It's no an exaggeration tae say he'd no be here now if eh hadn't helped him oot,' George adds, surprised at how defensively the tone of his words have become. When shove comes to barge he will back his twin to the hilt despite his obvious misgivings.

' Sorry George, eh didn't mean tae sound negative towards him or you or your lives, I just feel fir yi cos he ken it's no been easy. I just meant that that wisnae the way eh, or you, must've seen your life panning oot. When you say that he wouldn't be here, what dae you mean? Did he totally lose it?' he replied inquisitively, fishing for more despite George's apparent reluctance to engage.

' Well saying that he took it badly is just aboot the understatement of the century as far as em concerned. That was it fir him, his life basically ended, he never returned to work, the office wis left as he left it the night he went doon tae find the letter she'd written telling him she was leavin'. Clients queued up at the door and naebody arrived tae see them. Yi can imagine the scene- ah the minks fae Dundee waiting tae be defended for robbin RS McCalls in Reform Street and the lawyer they thought wis gonna get them off was posted missin in his hoose.' George explained almost affording a rueful smile to pass his lips as he stares into the middle distance in stunned reflection.

' Jesus, that must've been just pure mental! Eh wouldn't think they'd be the most sensible collection of people that you could set yir eyes on!' Alan said, feeding off his old friend's slightly softening features.

' Anyway, that was it fir him,' George interjected, returning to his default, ' he literally never left his hoose fir years efter that. And eh mean years. The shame wis too much fir him. He left just once and that wis tae fling all the possessions belonging tae Mary in the coup. He literally took everything she owned, put them in aboot fifty black bin bags and flung them in the dump and that was it, he was gone fir years. Naebody saw him and beh years, eh mean years.' George's voice gave the slightest hint of a croak, his stoic nature betraying him

89

for a second before he recovered his composure fully, displaying the front he has pushed forward for as long as he can remember. ' So yeah, it is fair tae say that he struggled a wee bit eh? The poor bastard,' he added somberly. Looking directly into Alan's eyes he noted how the years had given them knowledge, experience and a knowing glare that can only come with time. There was no suggestion that Alan was judging him or even being overly sympathetic, he was just listening. He was interested and George took solace from his keen ear and understated disposition.

' So did he literally just bide in the hoose ah the time then George? Never leave it at ah? That's a shame fir hi eh?' Alan asked inquisitively.

' Eh, he was too ashamed tae be seen in public. He couldn't even leave the hoose, no eve fir a minute. It was frightening. The only time he'd go oot wis tae get the messages and even then he's go incognito, hiding under a hat and scarf. He literally thought that everyone was lookin' at him or talkin' aboot him, he was paranoid basically. Fir weeks and weeks, me and oor mither would go around and shout through the letter box to try tae get a response but nothing happened. We'd even leave notes but they just joined the massive pile of unopened letters at his front door. Then things took a turn fir the even worse, if that was at all possible.' George mused, taking a large gulp out of his pint.

' Even worse? How is that even possible?' Alan exclaimed.

' Well, as eh said tae yi the other night, Eck was a real mummy's boy and she was distraught that he would not even open the door to her. She really thought that she could snap him oot oh his misery if she could just get to talk to him, but there wis mare to it than that. She was ill, terminally ill we the big C. She had been hiding it fae me and Eck in particular because she didnae want to add to his woes. She shouted through the letter box telling him that she had something important to tell him and that she was ill and she even left a letter pleading with him to come to visit her before she died, but he never responded. Eh learned later that he would put hear plugs in when we arrived at the hoose and that he would no even open the letters til after mum's death,' George says staring darkly down at the table in front of him.

' So how did he hear aboot it?' Alan asked.

' Whar do yi think? The death notices in the bloody Courier. Ironic or what? I think that was the start of his obsession we the funerals and findin oot wha was died everyday. In a way I think he goes to these funerals as a way of continuing his grieving for mum. He was utterly devastated that he wisnae there when she passed away and eh think he takes pleasure in grieving as the time tae make up fir it,' George suggested mournfully.

' Jesus wept Geordie, that's tough. Nae wonder he's such a sensitive so and so, he's no half had a lot tae contend we in his life. Now, eh dinnae mean tae change the subject so quickly but it is nearly a quarter tae three, we best drink up and head doon tae Dens eh?' Alan said, draining the life out of the dregs of the black stuff.

' Eh, let's go. Let's pray we'll get an entertaining game,' said George hopefully, dragging himself to his feet with his walking stick…..

Alexander continues to peruse the Dispatch section of his early edition of the Courier newspaper, as the sun tries vainly to outwit the collection of cirrus clouds that engulf it. Never can Alexander forget the heart wrenching moment when he saw the notice of his own mother's death in print. It was no way for a son to learn of his beloved mother's passing. Every time he creases open the paper, he can see those words etched in black, bold indelible ink slap, bang at the forefront of his mind: Pace, Catherine, retired school teacher and dear wife of the late George Brian and loving mother of twin sons Alexander and George Junior. Catherine passed away peacefully following a short battle with illness. The funeral service will take place at Mary Magdalena's Church and thereafter in the Invercarse Hotel. Family flowers only please, however kind donations to Cancer Research with be gratefully accepted.

No words have ever hit a man so hard and Alexander quite literally dropped the cup of tea he had just poured himself and crumbled to his knees, wailing and screaming for his loss. He could never forgive himself for dismissing his mother's hollering at the door and the fact that he never got to say goodbye to her before she died is a cross that he will never have the ability to bear. The funeral service and subsequent wake at least allowed Alexander to temporarily reverse his self-imposed reclusion, but straight away he returned to his hermit's ways. George never gave up on his brother, though, and years of cajoling and gentle prodding ultimately saw Alexander take tentative steps back into society.

Today, he has reached the 'R' section with a sense of frustration beginning to overwhelm him. Twenty death notices down and not the merest hint of a hit or even the most tenuous connection, ' How the heck could nobody I know have not died over the past few days, it just doesn't seem fair,' he mutters to himself, uncrossing and crossing his legs in opposite order in an effort to comfort the limbs that he believes are ailing. ' Now, who is next: Robson Steven, 25. Tragically and suddenly. Much loved son, grandson and brother, too soon departed and always to be cherished and never to be forgotten. No, don't know him,' Alexander whispered to himself, exhaling a sympathetic sigh. ' Such a young age to lose your life,' he considers, shaking his head.

Alexander considers his own life as a young man of the tragic Steven Robson's age and how, at that time, he viewed the future with spectacles tinted with gold. Everything was ahead of him- he had the world at his feet, an intelligent, erudite young man with the pretty love of his life on his arm and a degree in law that would pave his path the comfort and indulgence for the children he hoped he would rear. He remembers at school, reading the F. Scott Fitzgerald novel 'The Great Gatsby' and how he was struck by the essence of glamour and illusion so powerful that it teased and tantalized him into considering it the greatest love story of his, or any other, time. He was awe struck at the eponymous Gatsby who gave his name to the book and how popular and fabulous he was. He pictured himself affording friends the type of hospitality that Gatsby did in his superb Long Island home that gave the most amazing, ebullient soirees. But unlike Alexander, Gatsby seemed to be a man without a history, without history; whose eyes were always searching the glitter and razzamatazz for something, someone. Alexander had found his something, his someone, his life was mapped out in front of him until, like Gatsby, fate unwrapped it for him.

The final paragraphs of the novel are imprinted on his brain, not least because his teacher would make him learn in rote the quotes for analytical unpicking, but because their meaning resonated so strongly with him:

' Gatsby believed in the green light, the orgiastic future that year by year recedes before us. It eluded us then but that's no matter- tomorrow we will run faster, stretch out our arms further …… and on one fine day-

' So we beat on, boats against the current, borne back ceaselessly into the past.'

For Alexander, his own future eluded him. It starved him of his want and ability to stretch further, run faster as he battles to  stay afloat against a tidal wave of  gnawing memories that he has nearly drowned in. Now, he must retain some hope that tomorrow might bring some form of hope and that he doesn't succumb to the ultimate decline suffered by Gatsby in a tale that has long haunted and tantalized him in equal measure.

Then it hits him like a runaway freight train, the moment that will

shift his future forever. It is his green light to the future or red light from the past that shines directly out of the page and burns a hole in his elderly eyes. Each black letter flows together to form the words he has feared, dreaded and secretly looked out for over seemingly interminable years. Inside he had no idea how the words would hit him, if and when the reality of them struck, but the feeling that he has been thumped across the chest by a sledgehammer is not one that he had entirely discounted. On first read his eyes struggled to keep pace with his brain, scanning words in blind panic. On second read, he took additional care to devour the severity and reality of each word to convince himself that these were words written in the real world and not figments of his imagination:

' Stryde (nee Farrelly), Mary, 71 years old. Peacefully at home after a long and brave battle with cancer. Treasured wife of the late Darren, mother of Janet and cherished grand-mother of one much loved grand-child. She will be sadly mourned and was deeply loved, admired and remembered by her wider family and all who knew her. Cremation to take place on Monday at the Perth Parish Church. Bright clothes. Family flowers only, but if desired, donations will be greatly appreciated and welcomed by Cancer Research UK.'

A single, salty tear meandered down Alexander's wizened cheek, leaving behind a glistening trail before dropping ceremoniously onto the paper and blurring the news of his ex-wife's passing forever on the page. His mind has raced uncontrollably into a state of incomparable tumult. Alexander has no idea what the tear represented or how he is feeling, or, indeed, how he should be feeling for that matter. He briefly considers tearing the paper up, ripping it into a thousand pieces and dispatching it into the dustbin and out of his mind forever. After all, what happened to Mary Farrelly had no bearing on his life now and had not done so for decades. However, calm analysis is his default and his mind quickly turns to logic. His lawyer training directs his mind towards unpicking and analyzing the words on the page that his mind is struggling to come to terms with.

The journey through the words is an insane roller coaster of emotional turmoil.

Firstly, there is the seething rage and incandescent fury of seeing the words Mary and Stryde side by side in matrimonial black and white. It is that very combination of the two individuals whom he had loved so dearly that had precipitated his own seemingly terminal decline. The words late and Darren bring a similarly unsympathetic response, 'so the bastard kicked the bucket eh?' he sneers to himself, ' he got what he deserved, nothing trivial I hope. I missed that one in the papers.'

The words, 'Mother of Janet and grandmother of one,' provoke questions of curiosity and pinches of regret: how old was the daughter? Did she look like Mary? Was the grandchild a boy or a girl? Mary had always wanted a girl, a daughter to look after and grow old with, but then so had he, she should have been his not that bastard Darren Stryde's offspring. He didn't deserve to procreate. He imagines how his own mother would have doted on a granddaughter of her own, but never got the chance to. So it seems that Perth's where they ended up, where they fled to from him in secret during the dead of the night and without a spoken word? Out of sight, but not out his mind. How ironic that he should learn of this pair's ultimate demise through a collection of written letters when, to him, they had ended the quality of his life through the same cowardly medium. Then there is the, 'Bright colours.' Bright bloody colours? What is she demanding that we are all happy, fake cheesy smiles to celebrate her life. If only she'd considered the darkness she had brought to his life, a darkness that no garishly coloured Hawaiian shirt can mask.

His mind a concoction of conflicting emotions and a strange hazy blur of nothingness, Alexander rises to his feet and looks out as the sun peeks shyly out from the constricting confides of the sky cloudy pallor. A single shaft of sunlight illuminates a small fishing trawler which is heading westwards in the diminishing wind up the River Tay in the direction of Perth's fair city. In a moment of clarity the concluding words from 'The Great Gatsby' tumble back into the forefront of his mind, ' So we beat on, boats against the current, borne back ceaselessly into the past.'

With that, Alexander Pace turns about and, head bowed, walks off slenderly, languidly back in the direction of the Riverview Nursing and Retirement Home. Nobody ever knew who Gatsby was. Nobody knows what Alexander Pace will become.

# 13

## BACK 'HOME'

' By God, that was one Hell of a game Geordie boy,' Alan exclaims like an excited schoolboy. ' A last minute winner against United in the first match o the season? It disnae get any better than that! This is oor year eh reckon. United must be pure seek efter that,' he continues apace.

' Dinnae get ahead o yesel Alan,' George says bringing a sense of realism back to the situation. ' We've been here before, beating United is great, but knowin' Dundee we'll probably lose away tae St Mirren on Tuesday night and we'll be back to square one.'

The two old men are hobbling up Provost Road which, in their advancing years, provides a challenge the equivalent of scaling the north face of the Igor. The clock at the bottom of the Hilltown is creeping towards five bells and the sun is now casting a welcoming sheen on the pavements which are thronged with fans from both sides of the divide, whose rivalries and opinions are set to be traded in the local hostelries. Songs are being sung, hands are being clapped and emotions are running high, but there is no sense of unease or undercurrent of trouble brewing beneath the surface.

' Now di yi fancy one or two in Whites at the tap o the road tae pick the bones oot the gem George? My treat,' says Alan breathlessly, fumbling around in his pocket for the change that lies loose. He picks out a tattered 5 pound note that looks like it's been hibernating in there for most of the millennium and waves it in front of George's face as if it were a state lottery win.

' Eh better no Alan, but thanks anyway. Eh'd better get back to the home and see how the brother is, see what kind o bother he has in store for me noo,' says George reluctantly denying himself an extension to his day out.

' Eh, well, if yir sure. Em gonna pop in there for an hour or twa anyway, a few oh boys fae the Lochee Dark Blues Supporters' Club are meeting in here so eh'll catch up we them. You go ahead and see Eck. Eh've put him through enough for one week!' he adds giving George a knowing wink and a heavy pat on the back.

' You said it! Eh'm just gonna get this bus at the tap oh the road, the number 20 which terminates at Ninewells Hospital. They come at ten past the hour, so it's just aboot perfect timing fir me,' George says checking at his watch.

With the firm grip of a handshake the two elderly friends go their separate ways, promising each other that they'd meet again soon for another game in the name of fun and sociability.

George leans on his walking stick aboard the disabled seats of the number 20 bus and heaves a heavy outward sigh, partly inspired by his trek up Provost Road, but due to his mind switching to what might await him back at the Riverview Nursing and Retirement Home. The hectic day and the excess walking sticking has also taken its toll on his ailing limbs, though to that he would never admit. He exhales an exaggerated yawn as the bus circles the roundabout leading down towards the Hilltown clock.

Consumed with nostalgia, George leans into his back pocket and retrieves his brown leather wallet, pausing momentarily before gingerly pulling out a smoky coloured piece of paper which is crumbling to the point of disintegration at its folding points. At some parts the written words are utterly indecipherable to the untrained eye, but George certainly does not lack training in this sport, he could recite the 236 words backwards with his eyes closed, but just being able to see Angie's handwriting somehow makes him feel closer to her. He knows that one day the words will fade to nothing along with his memories of their blissful times together. Until then, the words fill him with the oxygen of hope:

*Dear George,*

*It is through tears and the most enormous feeling of regret imaginable that I feel compelled to write these words. Please do not think that this is a decision I have taken lightly. I can assure you with all my heart that it isn't, but it is one that I have to do for myself. I have given you the choice to come with me, but you have elected to stay and look after your brother and that is something I cannot and will not have a go at you for- he is family and needs you now more than ever and it is right that you cannot leave him on his own and break his heart further.*

*As you know, this chance for me to move to London is a once in a lifetime and I have to take it. I have to pursue my career and being in Dundee won't allow me to do that. It is not too late for you to change your mind though George, my train leaves at 11.00 tonight, it's the overnight train to Kings Cross. If you have a change of heart and want to come with me you can meet me on the platform.*

*If you are not there, I will accept that we are over and we'll have to sever contact because I won't settle there if we write to each other. I have to set up a new life down there with or without you. I admire your loyalty to Eck and he needs you now and I will understand whatever decision you make and will always love you. Please take care of yourself and that brother of yours and perhaps one day we can be back together again where we truly belong.*

*Your best friend and loving fiancé. Forever yours.*

*Angie.*

' Perhaps one day we can be back together again where we truly belong.' Thirteen words that he has vainly clung to since the day that he read them. But deep down he is aware that, with each passing year, just as the ink diminished from the page, so did the chances of their paths ever intertwining again. But clung he did, and cling he does, 'Forever yours' she said, forever hers he is.

Through waves of nostalgic fury, in pangs of angry spite George secretly curses his twin brother for his relationship's demise, he knows that he would have never had the chance to make up for lost time given that the decades that have gone dwarf the remains of his life's time. But would he change anything? If he could wind back the clock, would he adjust the future by allowing his twin brother to sweep up after himself and tidy up the wreckage of his own life? When he looks at his brooding, trodden reflection in the mirror and asks himself those questions, his answers are always 'no, he shares the same flesh and blood.'

As the number 20 trundles and juts through the city centre's cobbles, George stares, glassy eyed out of the window and into the middle distance, ignorant to the diverse assortment of individuals who stalk the city's Saturday evening streets. He notices not the red haired newspaper vendor selling the Evening Telegraph or the downtrodden Big Issue seller or the gang of youths gathered in hopeful menace or even scantily dressed women in skyscraper heels and ill-fitting boob tube tops whilst teetering their way into the night, or the drunken vagabond who sits outside Boots barking a raspy cough as he begs for more money to secure his next fix.

Despite his ignorance he considers that if he could he could peer inside the souls of this eclectic potpourri of people, if he could talk to them all one by one, he would doubt if he could unearth anyone whose past lurched so violently from love and success to an unsightly demise and downright desolation as that of his twin brother. The loss of his wife, his best friend and his business were too much for a man whose paper thin emotional shell was never likely to have the strength to withstand such a barrage of emotion sapping blows.

Gazing out of the window, George recalls like yesterday his twin brother in the throes of despair, spiraling from the lowest ebb to a rung the depths of which he had never seen plumbed. After their mother's funeral, Alexander crawled even further into his cocoon of self-loathing, holed up in his once salubrious West End abode which he allowed to run to rack and ruin through neglect inspired by depression. The house reflected Alexander's feelings, he cared for nothing or nobody, not least for himself who he despised more with every second that past, every wave that crashed violently and relentlessly against the shore. His loathing was borne out of the grief stricken heartbreak caused by those he should have been able to trust the most and the shame he felt for missing the passing of the one woman whom he was certain would never have let him down.

Paranoia and a crippling social phobia meant that Alexander became completely detached from the outside world. So much so that he didn't even allow the TV, radio or newspaper to communicate with him for fear that someone somewhere might be talking about him and his perilous demise. The business was sold ( at a significant loss) to an unscrupulous rival law firm which spotted the chance to secure the premises at a bargain basement price. Given the rumours that circulated about its incumbent's travails and mental state, taking advantage was like a hound snapping and snarling at the heels of a bewildered lamb. It was dog eat dog and Alexander was a petrified puppy. Alexander blamed himself entirely, cursing his stupidity and sense of failure so much that he became paralysed by a panic which manifested itself in the most crippling attacks of anxiety one could ever imagine. His door was locked, bolted, locked again and bolted further. Only Doctor Dawson would pass the peephole inspection, providing furtively futile pills which succeeded only in dulling the senses of a man whose senses needed a jump start into reality. George remembers how powerless and bereft he felt, how he tried with increasing toil and desperation to communicate with the brother he loved so dearly deep down. He would camp in his garden waiting for him to come out, scream into his letter box, even cry on his doorstep shedding tears so rare that they would come in floods as if they had been stored away since childhood in expectation of such a fall.

Inside a house of horrors, Alexander was living out a constant battle between mind and body but existed almost entirely under anxiety's strangling spell. He felt as though he was living in a swirling, panic controlled cocoon with the sword of Damocles perched permanently around an inch above his long, thin neck. In a small segment of the brain capable of deciphering irrational thought from downright madness, he knew that how he was acting made no sense at all, but he could do nothing more to fight it. He felt as though something had high jacked his power for rational thought and was holding it hostage. Nobody, not even the twin brother who was trying so desperately to pay the ransom fee, could set it free. It was not that he was suicidal, though two small scars he bears on each of his wrists give rise to the notion that, at times, those feelings lurked behind a dark corner not too far away. He was just sick of the life he had found himself in; a fate worse than death, a fate he felt powerless to escape.

With bills mounting and his mortgage in arrears, bailiffs were threatening Alexander's home. The money he had made from selling the business had been servicing the mortgage in the absence of any other income. When the banks contacted George as his next of kin, it became a seminal moment. In a fit of rage, George broke into the house in the dead of a winter's night when Alexander would be least prepared to shrug him off. Battering open the door with a wrench and a claw hammer, he would never forget the scene that awaited him until his dying day. The house was in a state of utter disrepair, the dank smell of unwashed clothes and body odour combed his nostrils as he entered, the backdraft knocking him off his already unsure stride. Wading through years of unopened mail he negotiated the winding staircase, tripping on clothes that littered the threadbare tartan carpet.

He knocked on his brother's bedroom door with a feeling of untold trepidation. When a further two, three, four, five attempts and accompanying calls went unanswered he barged his way in. Under the duvet of the bed he once shared with the woman he had loved lay a skeletal figure that George could barely recognise as his own flesh and blood. Only his head was visible, but George was struck by the utter thinness of Alexander, the skin clinging to protruding cheekbones and his Adam's apple reverberating in his gnarled neck as he snored gently, his thin, pale bottom lip twitching slightly. Instinctively George checked the bedside cabinet and saw a white medicinal bottle with the words Strong Sleeping Tablets on the front. In a panicked fear of the worst, he dived onto the bed, shaking his brother violently until he awoke in terror.

' Wh…, wh…., wh…. what are yo…y….yo…you   doing here George,' Alexander wailed, his unusually large, terrified eyes consuming his frail countenance.

' Em here tae sort your life oot ya daft bugger. Now get yir arse oot that bed this second before I kick it oot. Eh should've done this years ago. We need tae talk and eh'm no leavin' this midden until we sort this mess oot. And by mess I mean you and the hoose,' George barked, his eyes welling up in tears as he held his twin brother's emaciated shoulders in his strong hands.


Alexander's head dropped. It was tough to know if it was recognition, shame, regret or acceptance. What he wouldn't dare to do anything was deny his brother's request. If not for the sake of peace, but for the sake of his own well-being.

## 14

## SHOCK AND JOE

George alighted the bus at the stop around a hundred yards away from the Riverview Nursing and Retirement Home. He glanced at his watch and was thankful to see that he had missed dinner time; the steak pie from the match had filled him up sufficiently and he could think of better things to do than to 'share feeding time with the geriatrics,' as he would say.

Creaking open the door with his walking stick, he dismisses the offer of a kindly looking nurse who asks if he needs a hand along to his room. He looks around the living area, his eyes darting left to right to find his brother who he half expects to see playing chess with 'Old Joe', an ex-serviceman whose hearing has been diminished so badly by the sound of artillery that he can put up with Alexander's inanities, at least that is what George tells him.

Surveying the room, he sees Joe who is sitting impatiently with the board set up and the pieces unmoved, but there is no sign of 'Eck'.

' Eh bet that he is in the bloomin' computer room looking at that bloody funeral website or whatever yi call it,' he mumbles to himself. 'Old Joe', naturally, doesn't hear him. The usual suspects are relaxing after their Saturday night dinner and settling in for a night with the octogenarian's favourites: Ant and Dec and Vernon Kay's Celebrity Family Fortunes. Although, with the world championship snooker on BBC 2 from 8 o'clock, there could be some elderly blood spilled in the battle for control of the remote.

As George passes through he sees Lizzie, an elderly woman sitting in the corner wearing a knitted pink cardigan and brown knee length skirt, her expression fixed in a glaze as it always is. Her husband Gerald, a cheerful looking man with tramlines of silver hair that astride a sun beaten and bald head, is perched on one knee in front of her as he holds and rubs her hands and looks into her eyes with the most heartfelt look of love that one man could share with another. Lizzie's Alzheimer's is growing increasingly worse and her health is deteriorating fast, but Gerald never misses a day.

' She worked in a clothes shop in the town on the Murray Gate that's not there anymore,' Alexander once told George about Lizzie. ' Gerald told me that one day when he was in to see her, they really are a lovely couple. He said that he went in one day and she asked him if he needed any help and it hit him straight in the heart, love at first sight. He went in and bought himself three pairs of trousers that week, pretending each time that they were too big or small so that he could see her again. The sixth time he went in he asked her out and she said yes.'

Now Lizzie doesn't always know Gerald when he comes in, but he looks forward to seeing her every single day. Every day he introduces himself to his wife as though it is the first time that they have ever met. But his glass is more than half full, 'I'm lucky,' he has said to Alexander, ' I get to fall in love with her 365 days of the year and every day for the rest of our lives. Here's the thing, people see a couple of dithery old things, fools in fact, caught in a time warp waiting to die while looking all sad and wrinkly. They find it hard to believe that we would miss each other when we are gone, that we love each other without condition. But when I look at her I see the picture that I saw that first day, a picture that developed into a beautiful girl who wanted to spend her life with me. And that is it, that is what I will see forever.'

George vividly recalls these words as he corrects Gerald's walking stick, which has slipped absent mindedly onto the floor as he comforts his ailing wife. Gerald does not acknowledge George's act, not because he lacks appreciation, but because he is so transfixed in the eyes of his wife, ' Don't feel sorry for me,' he told Alexander, ' Or Lizzie, because we have had the best life that we ever could have had and you know why? Because we spent it together.'

Witnessing the selfless couple enjoy what might be approaching their final memories together strikes a chord with George, his feeling is not envy, it's regret. He would have died, literally, to see the love of his life again and he imagines what she might be like now. Is she still alive? Has she struggled like Lizze? Would she remember him? Is she in the full of her health? In any way, if they were together, he would have loved and cherished her, looked after and adored her more, even more than Gerald does Lizzie he believes. At least equally so. As his walking stick leads him through in search of his brother, he cries inside, silent tears for Lizzie and Gerald and for an angelic Angie who slipped him by.

George's progress is stopped just in front of the computer room by Nurse Mabel, who, to his eyes, is sporting a disposition that is as sunny as it usually is, but somehow seems to be masking news he may not wish to hear.

' George, it is great to see you back,' she says stroking his left arm timidly and offering him a sympathetic, closed eyed nod. ' How was the game? I heard that your team won, you must be delighted,' she added with attempted enthusiasm but minimal knowledge.

George, if he would admit it, has warmed slightly to Nurse Mabel. He appreciates the job that she has done with his twin brother, pandering to the needs that he so desires, but helping to drag his mind back close to the straight and narrow that it should be. He is trained in her responses and detects that something might be wrong.

' Is he ok? Whar is he Mabel?' he says, using her name for the first time he can remember, but nor prefixing it like his brother does, a sign that she needn't think that George respects her too much.

' Yes, he's ok George, but I'm afraid he's had a bit of bad news,' Nurse Mabel says sincerely.

' Ah, dinna tell us, he's been on that bleedin' website again and found oot that some bloke he met aboot fifty years ago doin' his messages in Asda in Kirkton has kicked the bucket,' George said incredulously.

' No, it is more than that George. He is in the computer room, just there,' she points, ' come on George, he has had a wee bit of a shock and has been asking for you so let's go and see him.'

George, normally repelled by the prospect, accepts the offering of Nurse Mabel's cocked left arm and heads off with her in the direction of the computer room. As they approach, they can see the lithe silhouette of Alexander shadowing against the back wall as the computer monitor stares brightly into his face.

' Eh'll be ok fae here,' George urges Nurse Mabel, freeing his arm reluctantly with a pursed lipped nod.

' No bother George. Now look after that brother of yours would you,' Nurse Mabel added, drawing a rare shared nod of the head from George. But somewhere inside Nurse Mabel's words resonate with him, his brother clearly needs looked after.

' How are yi Eck? Have yi had a good day? What are you looking at here?' he asks, pointing at the screen that lights up Alexander's face. His brother stares resolutely at the screen in front of him.

' Has somebody died Eck?' George says tentatively, his slightly quivering tones reflecting the worry that lies dormant within him.

' Not just someone, George. Not just anyone. Look at the screen.' Alexander beckons his twin brother forward. Deep down his brother knows what he is about to read, he has waited years to hear the news but he has never known how he, or more saliently, his brother, would digest it. But there it is on screen right in front of his eyes, as clear as any font could make it:

' Stryde (nee Farrelly), Mary, 71 years old. Peacefully at home after a long and brave battle with cancer. Treasured wife of the late Darren, mother of Janet and cherished grand-mother of one. She will be sadly mourned and was deeply loved, admired and respected by her wider family and all who knew her. Cremation to take place on Monday at the Perth Parish Church. Bright clothes. Family flowers only, but if desired, donations will be greatly appreciated and welcomed by

Cancer Research UK.'

George stares at the web page for a few seconds, his mouth slightly agog. He has prepared for this moment, his mind training him for how he might feel, but now that the moment has arrived he has no idea how he actually feels. In truth, his mind is churning through a kaleidoscope of emotions; relief, sadness, pity, anger, regret and, perhaps most pertinently, potential freedom from the constrictions of the past. But he knows his emotions are secondary right now and he places a strongly, conciliatory right hand on his twin brother's skeletal shoulder, squeezing softly what little muscular tissue he can find.

Alexander sits, his face consumed in a vacant, rheumy eyed glaze. George looks at his brother from a sideways angle, his eyes boring a hole in the sides of his cheek, but feels incapable of deciphering his brother's feelings based on his disposition. It will be a case where words shall speak louder than actions he feels.

' Well Eck, how are you? Eh guess this day was always gonna come eh?' George offers tentatively trying to gauge his reaction to the news.

Alexander considers his response and with a slightly quivering lip offers this: ' My wife is dead, but she died years ago in my mind at least. She was his wife in the end, that bastard who ruined my life.' His tone reveals a rare steeliness and an undercurrent of simmering anger that has eaten away at him like a cancer for decades.

' In a way, this might help you tae move on Eck, the fact that she's no around any mare, neither o them. The twa people wha caused yi a this bather have both died noo so maybe it's time to move on?' George suggests.

' Move on? How can I move on, my time has been and gone, they took away everything from me; the best years of my life, the chance to have a family, a home to be proud of, a business, everything.

Those years can never come back so there's nowhere to move on to. My time is coming to the end and I'm happy to see it out in here where there's nobody to bother me.'

' You might think differently over time Eck. This is very raw for you,' George responds hiding a grimace.

' You know, the only person I feel sorry for in this is her daughter-Janet the paper says her name is. She has been deprived of both her parents now. I bet she has no idea of the devastation her parents caused. I doubt she even knows that I exist. That pair will have deleted me out of their lives for ever, playing happy families with a daughter who should have been mine,' Alexander seethes as he briefly allows his mind to wander.

' Eck, it will dae you no good tae look back in anger. Yi ken what eh think? Eh think yi should go to the funeral on Monday. Eh think that will bring you some sense of closure,' George says, tip toeing the idea out.

Alexander's eyes remain fixed on the computer, he declines to even acknowledge his twin brother's suggestion. The mere thought of attending the funeral of Mary Farrelly being enough to invite the onset of anxieties he has fought tooth and nail to quell. This is one funeral he has no intention of crashing.

A bleeping noise emanating from the computer's speakers interrupts the uncomfortable silence which has hooded the room, turning both men's eyes in the direction of the monitor as an orange coloured, pixelated envelope appears on the bottom left of the screen with the words, ' Message received FAO Alexander Pace on rip.co.uk. click here to read.'

Alexander regularly receives messages from the website's forum, a facility for fellow mourners to exchange heartfelt sympathies and condolences with each other so this type of message is not uncommon to him. However, coming as it does on the day that the death of his ex-wife is announced, he is immediately consumed by a feeling of dread and trepidation.

George immediately recognizes his brother's fears. ' What's the matter Eck? Are yi no gonna open the messages? Wha is it fae?' he prods.

' I don't know George and I don't know if I want to know. Who could be looking for me? What do they want? Does someone know about Mary and I from the past,' Alexander says, his mouth visibly shaking as all the old feelings of paranoia start to tumble back slowly into his mind.

' It's probably just another one of yir buddies banging on aboot a funeral they've been at the day and how nice the cakes were at the wake. Come on, ease yir mind and open the message,' George's light hearted tone tries to lighten the mood.

' Oh, ok. I guess you are right George, it's probably nothing.'

With a trembling hand, Alexander dangles the cursor's arrow nervously above the envelope, hovering in time for a few seconds before his right forefinger clicks down to open up a new entry from cyber space. Both brothers look anxiously at the screen, their eyes darting across the page from line to line as they read the message's content. They stop, trade a shared disbelieving expression before their eyes return back to the screen, neither properly able to digest what they see in front of them:

' Dear Alexander,

I hope this finds you well. I realise that this message will come as quite a shock for you, particularly if you have recently learned of my mother's passing. However, it was she who asked me to deliver this message to you after she had gone and I am carrying out her wishes.

It was only in recent years, since the death of my father, that my mother told me of the whole circumstances surrounding your marriage and subsequent separation and I am being one hundred per cent genuine when I tell you that my mother was filled with remorse and regret with the way that she and my father treated you. In actual fact, it was only in these years that I even learned of your relationship at all therefore I had previously been unaware of your presence in mother's life, otherwise, please believe me, I would have made a concerted effort to ensure that she tried to contact you in order for her to express her sorrow to you.

It was only in the years after my father died that she was ever really able to show these emotions. I think, having spoken to her on innumerable occasions about it, she felt unable to express these emotions while dad was still alive. In recent months she openly started to state her intentions to try to re-establish contact with you because there were things that she needed to say to you and apologies she would like to have made. However, she became too frail and ill to see this through.

I took the liberty and looked for you on Google while mother was starting the process of searching for you and saw you were a member of this site. I know that this will all come as a major surprise to you and I sincerely hope that you do not mind me contacting you directly, especially under these circumstances. My mother asked me to tell you that she would dearly love you to attend her funeral service and I have an envelope that she gave me before she died that she wants you to have. It contains something private, she said, that she has not made me privy to.

I, and she, will understand if you do not feel you wish to come to the funeral.

I really hope to see you there. Thank you.

Yours faithfully,

Janet.


You could knock the brothers over with the lightest of feathers, lift them back up and strike them down with fresh air. A sense of numbed shock has enveloped the confines of the Riverview Nursing Home's computer suite. Visually, it is difficult to tell whose face is presenting the more distinctive signs of shock- George's brow having furrowed even more prominently and Alexander's lower jaw is lying so loosely that it appears it may require the aid of machinery to reintroduce it to the upper jaw.


' Well eh never,' George is the first to react verbally. He can genuinely think of nothing better to say than something that, in all reality, actually means nothing.

' How dare she!' Alexander suddenly screams at the screen in a fit of pique so rare that George nearly jumps out of his brogues. ' How dare she use her daughter to try to make up for what she did to me and my family! The arrogant bitch just thinks that because she suddenly develops some morals on her death bed that I will come running to her funeral service. Arrogant bitch!' he shouts, tossing the keyboard with an aggressive right elbow and kicking the wall in front of him.

George is startled by their reversal of roles as he tries to play peacemaker, ' Now calm yirsel doon right noo Eck. It isnae worth getting this upset over,' he says calmly as he encourages his furious brother to sit back down. ' Now relax Eck, sit yir erse doon here again.'

Alexander's face is ashen in fury, his top lip curled over his teeth as he inhales and exhales the feelings of anger that have now consumed him to the very core of his being. Refusing George's invitation to be seated, he paws his brother's hand away before unleashing a final diatribe in the direction of the screen:

' After all these years, she didn't even have the decency to apologise herself. What kind of person would allow her daughter to do her dirty work for her? I'll tell you who. Exactly the same spineless fucking weasel who dumped her husband for his best friend by letter. That's who!' he bawls, storming out of the room past George and Nurse Mabel who has arrived in an attempt to quell the commotion.

George is startled, he could swear it is the first time that he has ever heard his brother swear. Ever.

' Is he ok George? That sounded pretty nasty. Even old Joe whose hearing aid was switched off could hear the racket. What happened?' Nurse Mabel asks.

' It's a long story Mabel and it is no fir me tae say the noo, but let's just say we've no heard the last o this,' George responds, logging out of Alexander's webpage and shuffling out of the room in lukewarm pursuit of his smarting sibling.

# 15

## SEEKING SOLACE

Alexander is seeking solace where he habitually hunts for it as he sits on his bench by the bandstand on Magdalen Green watching the bright full moon paint a silvery shadow on the River Tay. He knows that in times of consolation, all he has to do is to lift his head to the ever shifting sea. A delivery train trundles slowly onto the rail bridge and the shunting of its pistons briefly avert Alexander's focus from the fury that has engulfed him and he fixes his glistening eyes on the lights of the houses in Fife which shimmer like loose change in the dulling light. He looks at the lights and wonders what is going on in these houses- the suburban homeliness, mothers feeding new born babies, children coming home from games of football in the park, families laughing around the dinner table with Chinese take away meals, couples arguing, families grieving, alcoholics slyly swigging, junkies secretly belting up, worried teenagers social networking in their insular rooms, loners, fighters, a frustrated man screaming at his children who refuse to settle after bath time, a woman crying into her bedroom pillow. Alexander imagines how all sorts is taking place under the flickering lights of those homes across the water. He cannot see inside but he knows that most have something that he doesn't. He won't admit it but he knows it in his core. Looking across the water at the shimmering lights reminds him again of his favourite novel 'The Gatsby Gatsby.' The eponymous Gatsby would look from his glamorous house at a green light which shone from a lighthouse at the end of Daisy Dock. Gatsby believed that the light represented his dreams, dreams that were so close he could nearly grasp them. Alexander wonders what dreams he has for the future, how his idyllic ambling towards a better life has been rudely interrupted by the demons of the past, the green light he had been reaching for has turned to a dangerous red.

The letter from just before the grave has prompted and prodded at raw emotions that Alexander had hoped would lie dormant as he inched away his life in the non-threatening environs of the nursing home. But here he is now, the living result of a collection of bashed letters on a keyboard somewhere near Perth has provoked a battle in Alexander's mind to repel the feelings of panic and anxiety that once consumed him so badly whilst at his lowest ebb.

He dares not return to those mind numbing days, holed up in his decaying house in fear of the outside world and what its inhabitants thought of him. He is happy where he is now, why did she who should never be mentioned have to come back to hunt and to haunt him?

His mind turns to George and all that he has done for him, the sacrifices he has made for him to the detriment of his own life and loves. Has he ever properly repaid him? Ever properly thanked him? Probably not, he thinks, but George never wanted any thanks, he just does what he does without the wrapping paper and the pretty bows.

It was this stoic determination, Alexander believes, that gave George the will to drag him back from the precipice of a vertiginous and seemingly terminal decline. It was George who dragged his brother out of his house and to the doctor to face up to the social phobias, panic attacks and sense of impending doom that had consumed his ability to function. George worked around the clock; extra back shifts and night shifts to fund private treatment from a specialist Cognitive Behavioural Therapist at Fernbrae Private Hospital who rewired his brother's brain to deal with the anxiety. Alexander learned to realise why he was feeling the way he was. He learned 'how to change the wheel rather than worry about how you got the puncture' as his doctor would say. When Alexander came to realise that it was the symptoms of his anxiety that were causing him to panic rather than the situation that he found himself in, it was the starting point to his road to some sort of recovery. Alexander had been running from situations because he believed that the symptoms of anxiety were dangerous to him and others around him, so he simply ran from them, locking himself away from the outside world, building an increasingly unassailable battle with his own mind. The doctor encouraged him to challenge the symptoms. He told Alexander, ' Imagine that you war walking across the Serengeti and you see the grass rustling in the distance, you don't stand there and think "I wonder if that is a saber tooth tiger waiting to come and pounce on me," you run to safety, hide up a tree, whatever. But then you are supposed to look back to see if it really is a saber toothed tiger or just a domestic cat. Unfortunately, because you have not identified that it is the symptoms that are causing your issues, you have not been able to look back and are running and hiding from the real issues. You are not disturbed by the events, you are disturbed by your interpretation of them. You must run and hide no longer.'

This advice, funded by his twin brother and delivered sternly by a trusted quack, helped Alexander to gradually, very gradually take his first, tentative, tip toed steps back into society, but dealing with the physical manifestations was easier than healing the oozing psychological scars that hid behind them. But, Alexander knows, that the situation he has inadvertently found himself in just now- the predicament of whether or not to accept the backhanded invitation of his ex-wife's daughter to her mother's funeral after decades of abyss – represents that creature rustling ominously in the long grass of the Serengeti. The question is, does he run and hide from the saber tooth tiger or snuggle up to the domestic pussy cat that has helped heal a permanent nasty scratch?

' Eh thought eh'd find yi doon here. Here's yir jacket, it's a bi chilly,'

117

George's voice punctuates the shrill summer air from behind.

' Thanks George, there's an ill wind blowing right enough, in more ways than one,' Alexander says as his brother neatly places his brown sports' jacket over his shoulders, its arms hanging loosely by his sides and swaying slightly in the gentle sea breeze.

' Eh've been thinkin aboot it there Eck and yi dinna hae to take meh advice and yi can tell me tae shut meh puss, but I think you should go to the funeral. Eh ken that it sounds ridiculous that you would go to her funeral after all that she's done tae you, but if yi think aboot it, it will draw a line under everything once and for all. You can move on with yir life,' George says, sincerity dripping out of every word.

' Thanks George, I really do appreciate your advice. I have calmed down a little since that message appeared. I find that coming down here, just looking out across the sea, taking in this beautiful view really helps me to think a little straighter,' Alexander says turning to look at his brother.

' Eh, it is lovely. This always brings back memories fir me,' George says with a croak in his voice, ' That night eh got engaged doon here, eh could never have imagined in meh worst nightmares that oor relationship would turn oot like it has. Eh've never had the chance to draw a line under that relationship. Eh ken that Angie is still oot there somewhere and that breaks meh heart every time eh think aboot it, but it's too late now. This though is your chance Eck. She broke your heart a lang time ago and this is the chance for you to heal it, to get the ultimate closure. If yi go on Monday then there will be nothing left to the imagination. She will be gone and gone for ever and you will sit we yir ain eyes,' George urges, his voice rising in volume with emotion.

' Maybe you are right George,' Alexander concedes, ' I totally trust your advice because you have rarely done me wrong in that way in the past. I am just worried, worried sick that all those old thoughts and feelings will come flooding back. The negative, gut wrenching anxiety that I let get on top of me and nearly ruin my life. What if turning up on Monday is the catalyst for those dark days to come back? I'm happy with my lot just now George, happy at last, do I need this?' Alexander asks staring straight into his twin brother's eyes.

' But you have so much more to offer the world Eck than what you have the noo. This nursing home is ok, but there's mare tae life than sitting playin' chess we Old Joe or crashing bloomin' funerals. That's the world you have locked yourself into and you could be dayin' so much mare. We both could be and eh honestly think you will find that oot when we get a bit of closure, I am certain of that,' George urges straight from the heart.

Alexander chewed over his brother's musings in contemplative silence, breaking it some seconds later, ' Well maybe I will go to Mary's funeral then George. I'll take your advice after all. On one condition though.'

' What's that?'

' That you come too.'

' Eh, yiv dragged me tae every other funeral in the country so eh may as well come tae this one yi daft bugger!' The sound of the brothers laughing so heartily echoes eerily into the pitch darkness of the night.

' One more thing George. I'm sorry, I don't think I've ever said that enough,' says Alexander, interrupting the mood.

' Sorry for what?'

' Sorry for ruining your life.'

# 16
# JOURNEY

' Customers are reminded to always use the handrail and to take care on the stairs...... Customers are reminded to always use the handrail and to take care on the stairs......Customers are reminded to always use the handrail and to take care on the stairs......'.

As the screeching, high-pitched station announcement pierces the dewy summer air and into George's eardrums and Alexander's hearing aid, the twin brothers heed the unnecessarily repetitive automated advice like it was delivered from a higher power as they negotiate the stairwell of Dundee Railway Station with trepidation. George's squat frame and short bow legs struggle downwards as he holds the red handrail with one hand and grimly grips his wooden walking stick with the other. Alexander, having ambled down with his gangling strides, stands at the bottom of the stairs clutching his lower back with the downturned palms of both hands and inhales exaggeratedly to ensure George is aware of his imagined pain.

Though his physical ailments may be open to question, what cannot be denied is the fragility of Alexander's mind-set as he prepares to board the early morning commuter train from Dundee to Perth, a journey that will bring him to the funeral service of a wife who left him for his best friend all those years ago.

' That staircase is all I need, what with my ailing back, brittle bones and not to mention my nerves. George, I'll tell you, I think I will head back to Riverview now, I really can't cope with this,' Alexander whimpers as he wipes beads of perspiration from his increasingly furrowing brow.

' You'll dae nothing oh the sort,' George barks back like a breathless terrier, ' You've made it this far now so there is nae turnin back. Mind oh what that doctor said to you years ago, do you remember?'

' Wh.., wh.. what you mean? About the Serengeti?' stutters Alexanader.

' Eh, that's the ain.'

' He said to face your fears and that when you look back you will see that it was a domestic cat hiding in the grass and not a saber toothed tiger waiting to devour you,' Alexander said with closed eyes and inhaling large gulps of oxygen.

' Eh, you got it brother. This is just a trip tae Perth, there's nae saber toothed tiger waiting there fir yi. There may be a bitch, but that's aboot it,' George says half in joke.

Alexander ignores his brother crudity and takes the next of his tentative steps towards the platform, frantically batting away negative thoughts from his tumultuous mind. As they arrive, they stand in silence waiting for the train, George allowing his brother the chance to battle his own mind without interruption.

Without a glance in its direction, Alexander hears the train of destiny clatter and shunt closer; with it, his heartbeat quickens, thudding like a mallet on cloth against inner walls of sinewy chest. He slowly inhales, grasping for air to ease the tension. Inside the pocket of his brown suit trousers, his already ravaged nails scratch nervously on the cold clam of his palms and claw at what's left of the cuticle on his pinkie finger.

Without glancing up he feels a waft of muggy air flush over his reddened cheeks and in his peripheral vision he spots the train shuttling past to finally settle at the platform. He knows this is his time, time to board, time to face the demons that have (seemingly) forever consumed him. He lifts his trembling hand to his forehead again and gently rubs another thin lining of perspiration that has gathered like an unwanted ex at a party. Trying to pull himself together, he drags his feet pensively towards the train, following in the steps of the swathes of early morning commuters.

As George and Alexander reach the door, an avuncular looking man in a deerstalker hat  opens up the palm of his hand to encourage them to proceed him onto the train. 'No, after you. Please, I insist,' he says cheerfully imploring them ahead.

' Thank you sir,' George says and the brothers board the train to find a seat in the middle carriage. Alexander looks at the faces of other passengers- carefree students, a jaunty middle-aged commuter desperately trying to engage a stern looking woman in conversation, a suit reading a broadsheet newspaper, a tramp who smells like a child's nappy supping the dregs from a can of Tennants Super, nobody sitting or standing within three square yards of him. And then there they sit, George and his brother on the way to his dead ex-sister in law's funeral. ' It really does take all sorts,' he thinks to himself silently.


Alexander glances out of the Inter City 125's  dusty window and shades his darting, almond shaped deep brown eyes from the melancholic morning sun which is now reflecting perfectly on the River's Tay's ebbing silvery waters. He focuses his gloomy gaze on the beautifully constructed cast iron rail bridge which paints its own perfect picture on the still, glasslike water and the view encourages him to feel a momentary sense of calm. It's a similar view to the one he seeks solace from down at the bandstand on Magdalen Green, a picture that would be imprinted forever in his mind should he drop dead tomorrow. He thinks of the terrors the passengers on the train would've felt on the night of the 28th of December 1879 when the bridge's central spans gave way during high winter gales. Any good Dundonian knows the history of the rail disaster like the palms of their hands. A train with six carriages carrying seventy-five passengers and crew, crossing at the time of the collapse, plunged into the icy waters of the Tay. He imagines the grief of the victims' families, the abject terror of the drowning passengers and convinces himself that at some time, somewhere, there are many, many people far, far worse off than himself. For all his troubles and strife, he still has a foothold on the planet. For the first time in days he feels relaxation override his mind. He feels just about equipped to face up to whatever travails the day has in store. Just about.

17
## SERVICE OR DISSERVICE

Alexander steps leaden footedly out of the silver taxi that collected the brothers at the train station to deposit him and his twin brother at the gates of the Perth Crematorium. As always they had arrived as late as they conceivably could do  to the service, this time on the instruction of Alexander rather than George. Both men have ignored the request to wear brightly coloured clothes in celebration of Mary's life. For Alexander there is nothing to feel colourful about and George doesn't have a colourful item in his wardrobe.

His heart pounding and cheeks rumouring silently, Alexander exhales a heavy breath that subtly permeates the warm summer air and, with George in tow, he takes his first tentative step towards his first meeting with Mary in three gruesome decades. As his brown brogue shoes crunch on the gravel path, he removes a neckerchief from his inside pocket. He wraps it around his neck and pulls it close to his lower lip before slipping on a trilby hat which is closely introduced to his grey, neatly trimmed eyebrows. It is Alexander's attempt to go incognito. The brothers begin their walk up the leafy church lane as the cherry blossom leaves begin their trudge back from fullest bloom.

' Yi look stupit like that Eck, take them aff!' George whispered forcefully, ' It's the height oh summer and you have a scarf wrapped around yir neck. You will bring mare attention tae yisel like that than anything else. Besides yi won't ken anybody in here, she didnae hae any family tae speak of and the ones she did hae will be dead anyway. '

' Would you be quiet and let me deal with this my own way George. I do not want anybody seeing me here. I'm feeling nervous enough as it is without you nagging at me, now leave me be please,' Alexander pleaded his face ashen in fear.

' Ok, sorry. I'm just saying that...'

' Leave it, please now George, I beg of you. Now please, let's get this over and done with.' For once, George cannot offer any kind of riposte.

Alexander's quivering hand creaks the intimidating black door of the crematorium ajar. The door sighs open without so much as a creak and only the faint clinking of George's walking stick on the marble floor punctuates the cool draught as they quietly squeeze their way through into the main body of the kirk. The heads of people dressed in colourful colours are bowed to the backdrop of somber laments which hush mournfully from the organist's fingers and slowly step through the church.

Alexander nods his head to the left to indicate that he wants to sit in the back row, three or four pugs clear of any other mourners and they shuffle to their seats without the bat of any eyelids other than the four of their own. Restlessly settled, Alexander keeps his head firmly bowed, his Adam's apple struggling to consume bursts of saliva as his moist eyes stare downwards. His brown eyes blink occasionally, his glassy glaze like a windscreen wiper clearing a squally shower. But this is so, so much more than a squally shower to him, it is like a turbulent tsunami of pent up emotions repressed in his slender, elderly frame.

The minister, a rotund gentleman with a cheery disposition hidden beneath his somber façade stands erectly at his lectern at the top of the church. Five stairs below him is the shiny, faint brown wooden casket containing Mary Farrelly's body. The coffin lies closed, encapsulating the body and soul of a woman who has delighted and despaired the gathering bereaved in equal measure. Alexander's head remains bowed, staunchly denying himself of the inclination to look at the casket which symbolises the best of times and the worst of times.

' Ladies and gentlemen of the congregation, please rise' the minister says adjusting his position at the top of the church, ' We are all sadly gathered here today to celebrate the life and times of the much loved and cherished woman Mrs. Mary Stryde. Now, please be seated.'

Alexander visibly bristles in his seat, the combination of Christian and surname striking him like a stake in the heart. ' Stryde? Bloody Stryde! That should be Pace,' he quarrels internally, shifting uncomfortably along the glossy wooden pew. George sits resolutely next to his brother, trying his best to remain unmoved and unwavering

'Now for some words on the dearly departed. Mary sadly passed away on Wed July 5th, 2013 after a brave fight with an illness that she ultimately could not conquer. As we remember Mary as a kind and loving supporter of this congregation, our sympathies, thoughts, best wishes and all our heartfelt prayers go out to the family and friends that she has so sadly left behind, as well as those who have already departed.

' Particular thought must go out to her only child Janet and her grandchild Helen whom she so doted on until the day she died. We all know how broken hearted Mary was when her beloved husband Darren passed away just over 5 years ago and how she struggled to come to terms with her loss. However, the bravery that she showed in the throes of bereavement did not go unnoticed and the way that she stayed strong for the sake of Janet was an example to everyone.

' Those who knew Mary will vouch for the fact that her sense of loyalty and devotion were aspects of her character that were never in doubt...'

Alexander, mentally unpicking every morsel of the eulogy, shakes his bowed head slightly and slowly in utter disagreement as he feels his blood physically boil around his veins? His analytical mind focuses on the words 'loyalty' and 'devotion'. Loyal and devoted to everyone but himself he fumes.

126

For Alexander, it is the fight or flight syndrome. Does he face the animal in the Serengeti or does he obey the power of his thoughts which is urging him with all its might to run out of this church and not look back? Does he face the demons of the past or turn his back on them and place them on the long finger again?

' We all grieve in a special way today before the loving God of Heaven here in Perth. Mary was truly a lady after God's own heart and a person who changed the lives of everyone she met…' the minister continues.

' Changed my life alright. Ruined it forever in fact. I bet he doesn't mention that,' Alexander whispers to himself, his eyes narrowing into a crack in the floorboard beside his feet. The minister's words begin to fade in their significance for Alexander. Why does he have to listen to this? This is not the woman that he once loved and married is it? It is someone else, not Mary Farrelly or Mary Pace, but Mary Stryde. Alexander and everything he contributed to her life have been airbrushed from memory and that is where they will remain.

With the words of the minister now no more than a white background fuzz, Alexander goes to stand up and move out of Mary's life forever when his ears are pricked by, ' Now I'd like to invite Mary's daughter Janet to say a few words about her mother as she has bravely and kindly requested to do.' Suddenly, like having your name mentioned in the background noise of a cocktail party, he retunes in.

Alexander reengages his backside with the seat and, for the first time, he is tempted to raise his head above the parapet. His mind is urging him to look up, to catch a glimpse of the offspring of his late ex-wife, to see for himself the young lady who has invited him to share these final memories, the young lady who claims she has an envelope to hand him from beyond the grave and has implored him to collect.

Peering perilously from above the rim of his glasses, Alexander fixes his intent gaze on Janet, watching her every stride as she walks airily, but with a slow, nervous caution towards the minister's lectern.

Dressed in a bright red pencil dress with a neat, bright white collar to cover her tall, thin frame, Janet's black high heeled shoes clink elegantly on the marble church floor revealing a flash of red sole with every step, bringing a blink of colour and a solitary noise that filters breezily around a hushed place of worship. As she turns to face the colourfully dressed congregation, a lump develops in Alexander's throat and, as he gulps it free, it joins his heart in his mouth. Janet's face is slightly shadowed and cloaked by a tilted black and red hat as ringlets of red hair spill down each side of her face, faintly tickling the pink cheeks that sit on her pale, porcelain skin. Janet fixes her large, almond shaped, deep brown eyes on the back wall of the church and a single tear drips from her right eye, which she dabs with a tissue that she pulls with a thin, slender hand from the full length sleeve of her dress.

Alexander has joined George in becoming transfixed by the young woman who stands before them. The similarity to her mother is startling. In many ways she is the image of Mary around the time that she had so cruelly walked out on Alexander, but she has a more refined edge and her eyes draw in such feelings of sympathy that even Alexander finds it difficult to link the woman he sees before him to the deportment of the woman who ruined his life. As for Darren, he seeks to find nothing of him in Janet and, therefore chooses against recognizing any of the traits his loins may have gifted his offspring.

Janet clears her throat, clutching the lectern with her thin, pale hand to reveal the bony knuckles on her shaking hands. Emotion has etched a pained look on her face and her lips quiver slightly as she opens her eulogy:

' Firstly, I would like to thank each and every one of you for coming here today to pay your respects to mum, I am certain that it would have meant everything and the world to her to see so many familiar faces from past and present here today and I am sure that she is up there somewhere looking down on as all with a smile on her face,' Janet says in a well heeled central Scotland accent which is straining

128

with the raw emotion of bereavement.

' That is the thing about mum, no matter how difficult a time she was going through, be it the death of dad or her difficult battle with illness, she always had a smile which seemed to make even the worst of times seem just that little bit better. The memories that I will cherish most are the ones that I have of growing up and growing closer to mum with every passing minute, every day and every year up to the point where I can safely say that I have not just lost a mother, but I have also lost my best friend,' Janet continues, pausing briefly to gather her thoughts and encourage sympathy from the congregation.

' I know that from speaking to her in the recent weeks leading up to her passing, that she did not wish people to cry over her or to mourn her loss, but that she was thankful for the time that she had on this Earth and eternally grateful to all the people who contributed so much to her life.' She hoped that all of you will come to the hotel afterwards for a drink and some food where we can all celebrate the life of the mum we all loved so much. Thank you all so, so much from mum and I,' Janet concluded with a quivering voice.

Janet spoke with such an alluring and quiet dignity that the entire congregation sat captivated; some nodding, some weeping, some silently reflecting. There was calmness to her as she walked back to her seat, carrying herself with a steady grace and an air of sure footedness that belied her shaking limbs and churning sadness. There was no round of applause or haughty outward displays of emotions, just a wailing undercurrent of sadness that played out to the backdrop of the lamenting church organ which whistled Mary's requested tune 'Wind Beneath My Wings'. George and Alexander sat in reflective silence; the only movement was of George's eyeballs which he was straining to the right in an effort to surreptitiously see his brother's face. If he could have strained them further they would have witnessed a relaxed looking countenance which had seemed to have, temporarily at least, freed itself of the anxiety and stresses which had

129

been its constant projection. It was almost as if the sight of Janet, so bereft and consumed by bereavement and emotion, yet so incredibly dignified and assured had inspired a calmness in Alexander that had long been his enemy. If she could deal with such a situation with such assurance and appear to inspire others less fortunate, then who was he to bring everyone down into his own living hell? Never, even in his wildest nightmares or most perilous throes of despair, could Alexander Pace have envisaged finding even a modicum of inspiration from Mary's daughter whom he didn't know even existed. But, perhaps, just perhaps, her ability to stand up so gracefully, so bravely to the loss of the woman she loved as much as he once had might prove the catalyst for some realization that the fate better than life that he craves does not lie with mortality. These notions may not last, but they were rare and could at least be clung onto.

' I think we should just slip out quietly now and head off to the hotel early so that we can get a seat that is not too conspicuous. I have seen enough here and I'll go to the hotel to receive the envelope from her mother as she suggested I should,' Alexander whispered, nudging his elbow into his twin brother's bicep.

At Alexander's request, George agrees and the pair shuffle along the seats and silently slip unnoticed out of the door of the church without the turn of a single head from the mournful, colourfully attired congregation. As the imposing church door at the front of the crematorium whistles closed, the minister begins the next part of the service. Mary Farrelly, Mary Pace and Mary Stryde is set to depart this stage for the last time and the curtains will close on the final act of her life. The husband she left behind all those years ago closes the door of a taxi he has flagged down at the outside of the church and does not look back. Beside him, his loyal brother George sits in hope that a curtain can be drawn on the dim and dark past and reopened to a future with a more welcoming glow.

# 18
# UNION

' She was a credit,' Alexander mused, staring into the middle distance at a spot on the hotel suite's wallpaper. ' The manner in which she was able to stand there looking so composed, showing such raw emotion in such a dignified way was a real example of how to deal with the loss of someone, don't you think George?' he added as if reading from a prepared script in his mind, taking a large slurp from his lukewarm cup of tea.

' Eh, she did really well Eck, really caught the mood just right,' George nodded, loosening the grip of his black tie and unbuttoning the top of his shirt. ' The maist amazing thing was that she just looked the pure double oh her mother, especially with that red hair and everything, though she was a wee bit taller it has tae be said. Lovely lookin lassie though,' he added dunking his chocolate digestive into his cuppa.

Ignoring the reference to Mary, Alexander agreed, ' Yes, she has a lovely look. Very beautiful young woman. Those eyes just drew everyone in today. She has a charm about her, that's for sure.'

' Well she disnae take after her faither that's for sure. He was aboot as charmin' as a pound o mince,' George snorted. Again, Alexander chooses to ignore the baited jibe.

Sitting as far back in the right hand corner of the room as it is possible to be, the brothers nervously await the arrival of the other mourners to the wake. Alexander shuffles with a bar mat, flicking it over and back, his mind consumed with a tsunami of thoughts. He has shed most of his disguise, half in the knowledge that he had hardly known any of Mary's family and, even those whom he did know were bound to have kicked the bucket by now if age was any gauge. But his attitude had also softened slightly too, he felt slightly less tense, a little less apprehensive. Whilst he was far from embracing the occasion, he at least felt that he need not have to abscond from the place at the merest mention of his ex-wife's name.

As the somber swarm of mourners murmur and mumble their way into the hotel's function room, the brothers shift more uncomfortably in their seats. George trades half smiles and fleeting glances with glassy eyed bereaved, who politely accept the offer of cups of tea and various sundries and pastries. Gradually the noise of clinking tea cups and whispered tones increases in volume as people begin to reacquaint and trade memories of the departed.

Alexander, his memories blackened by ills of the past, looks over the eye line of the crowd to see the tilted black hat he has been waiting to spot, under which the ringlets of red hair are now more generously in view. As her pale, porcelain face emerges into clarity it represents, to Alexander, the antithesis of the dark days of the past. Hiding the scars of grief that are scratched and etched indelibly beneath the surface of her grieving countenance is a breezy disposition which Alexander regards, almost enviously.

He watches her intently for several minutes as she chats with mourners, holding their hands in hers, comforting some, smiling through cherished memories with others and all done with a demure decorum. Alexander sits, almost spellbound by her ability to deal with not just her obvious, but with the focus of that grief through other people.

' There's Janet there the noo, eh didn't see her comin in,' George says just spotting her through the crowd. Alexander does not even hear his brother, George doesn't even realise he has not been heard.

' Eh think she is comin' o'er here noo Eck, look there,' George adds, this time nudging Alexander's right arm with his left elbow whilst shuffling up in his chair and tightening his tie. Alexander doesn't feel even the slightest hint of a nudge, far less hear his brother's verbose verbal promptings.

The brothers watch as she weaves her way through the sedate gathering, exchanging pleasantries and memories with everyone she meets. Emerging from the assembled throng, she, for the first time, exchanges eye contact with Alexander. It is a look that lingers with a strange familiarity and is held by both as their eyes widen, narrow and blink in equal measure.

Alexander knows it is Janet because he saw her at the church eulogizing about her mother's passing, but he wonders how she knows it is him. He is not sure why, but he knows that she knows it is him. It may be the process of elimination, or the nervy look that has afflicted his disposition, or perhaps Janet's mother had described what her ex-husband had looked like all those years ago. But in any of those cases, or indeed any other case, she knows that it is Alexander Pace.

Still holding the gaze that seems transfixed with sadness, she quickens her side slightly, making a bee line for where the brothers are sitting, her high heels clinking with increased rhythm across the wooden floor. She stops just in front of the table and, tilting her head slightly she extends her thin right hand out, her left placed softly across her chest.

' You are Alexander Pace aren't you?' she inquires with a tentative assuredness.

Alexander rises uneasily to his feet, the chair on which he is screeches backwards as he frees his long limbs from under the table.

' I am surely,' he replies, his voice croaking ever so slightly. ' How did you know?' he asks, shaking Janet slowly by the hand, his palm clammy with the perspiration of emotion.

George remains seated and observant. Alexander bows his head slightly, just enough to miss the welling of tears in the eyes of Janet. She breathes in heavily in an effort to retain the composure that she had assured herself that she would maintain throughout this difficult day.

' You are just as my mother said you had looked like,' Janet said, a single tear escaping over the barrier of lightly applied mascara. ' She had also shown me some pictures of you recently and you have not change much at all. I knew that it was you the minute that I saw you there. You look exactly as I had imagined.'

Alexander digested her words quickly, efficiently. He wondered how she had taken the news of her mother's secret ex-husband, how she had reacted. He wondered why she had gone to the lengths late in her life to show her pictures, pictures he never imagined she would have kept, far less shared. He quickly figured that she had come clean to avoid her daughter finding out about her mother's actions posthumously. Nevertheless, Janet's words had surprised him, as had her emotions which he could tell she was straining every sinew of her being to stop escaping from her vent.

' Well, I have certainly changed a great deal since your mother last saw me, and in many more ways than one, but thank you nonetheless,' Alexander replied with a straight bat. ' Now Janet, this is my twin brother George,' he says nodding in his sibling's direction. George uses his walking stick to strain his creaking body erect.

' Pleased tae meet yi Janet. Pity it wisnae in better circumstances eh? Especially seein as we didnae even ken yi existed til a few days ago,' George says in a somewhat tactless Dundee brogue that he inadvertently hopes will ease emotions.

Janet, smiles through her dewy eyes, ' Yes, mother told me about you too George. It is really genuinely so pleasing to meet you, having heard so very much about you both over the past wee while.'

' Eh, well if yi dinna mind eh need tae use the wee boys' room so eh'll be back the noo  Eck,' George says patting his brother on the shoulder while making his excuses to leave Janet and Alexander alone.

For a brief second Alexander feels stranded, like a rabbit in the headlights, left on his lonesome to deal with a situation which would have been so preposterous in his mind all those years ago that he could never have even made it up. He internally curses George for leaving his side, the crutch that he has relied on for so long neglecting him in his time of greatest need. It is fight or flight again. But Alexander persuades himself to develop the steel to face up to this version of the Serengeti's saber tooth tiger.

After a shifting of feet and an uncomfortable interlude, Alexander breaks the silence by bringing the conversation back to first principles, ' Now, you must be aware Janet that this is extremely difficult for me and I am really just here for perhaps a little closure and to receive the envelope that you said had been left for me. I am still unsure if collecting this is the right call but I have decided to nonetheless. It may or may not prove to be against my better judgment,' he says looking directly into Janet's large, consuming eyes. He can see so much of her mother when he looks at her, but he tries desperately to avoid that line of thought and parks the notion to the back of his mind.

' I cannot thank you enough for coming today,' Janet says, visibly troubled by the additional trauma that meeting her mother's ex-husband has brought to her day. ' I know that you must have found this incredibly tough, but mother really wanted you to be here. She regrets nothing in her life other than the way that she treated you and the way that she failed to ever say sorry.' Janet accepts the offer of Alexander's tissue. Alexander remains quiet and passive, declining politely the offer of Janet's hand which she tries to place conciliatorily on his wrist.

' I am here because you asked me to collect an envelope and nothing more,' Alexander says looking through her. ' The fact that I am here should not be seen as an acceptance or a way of forgiving. It might help me move on. Perhaps. But you have to remember what that woman put me through and not a bean of an effort was made to put it right during her life.'

' You must believe me, I was absolutely appalled when mother told me what had happened, the way that she had mistreated you. I didn't think she was talking about herself but some other being. I can tell you with all of my heart that she was so, so, so sorry about it and regretted it until the day she died. She told me so only a few days ago. If I had known earlier I would have done something about it myself.' Janet's words are now diluted through flowing tears. She refuses Alexander's declination of her hand and grabs his thin, frail hand in her demure, soft palm.

' But Janet, I actually looked at you during the service and watched you in awe. I thought to myself that you were the embodiment of exactly what I thought that your mother would be and the opposite of everything that I saw that she became. I really thought that your mother would be like you- faithful, confident, content. Through the tears and tribulations I could see that you were all those things. What was your mother thinking about? I ask myself that question at least ten times a day. I never have come up with an answer,' Alexander wallows.

' I don't have the answer to that and neither did mother. Dad never let her talk about it, but the regret ate her up inside. Every day, she said, she wanted to find you to say sorry, but with every day that passed it became harder. Nevertheless,  dad wouldn't have countenanced it,' Janet said, clutching Alexander's trembling hand.

' He was a bastard. It was all his fault, I know it,' Alexander curses as he drags his hand back into his own possession in a rare outward fit of pique. Janet declines to comment, withdrawing her gaze from Alexander's moistening eyes.

' I am sorry Janet. I didn't wish to speak ill of your father, particularly now that he is dead, but his role in this mess merits my anger.'

' Listen,' Janet says reengaging, ' I totally understand your fury and I do not in any way condone what happened.'

' Did she love him like she loved me? Did she tell you that?' Alexander says visibly breaking down.

'This is not for now. Remember, he was a father to me and this is not the time or the place to be talking about these matters of the heart, it is all too raw, too emotional,' Janet replies with emotional sincerity. She clearly feels for Alexander, but is not allowing her emotions to betray her.

'Janet, I am so, so sorry. You're right, this is not the time and place to be talking about this, here where you are grieving. Continue the day and ignore me. Once George returns from the lavatory we will be off,' Alexander concedes, retreating into his shell.

'Don't forget though, I have the message that mother asked me to deliver you,' Janet says reaching into her silver and black handbag. She rustles around for a second before removing a pristine white once folded envelope from her diamond encrusted bag. Janet hands the envelope over, Alexander offers a fleeting glance to its front, noticing his name is scribed on it in the handwriting that he recognizes as a trembled version of his ex-wife's. Briefly his mind turns to the last envelope he opened written by her and bearing his name. He tries to bat the thoughts away, but he inwardly seethes as a snapshot image appears in his mind of him dropping to his knees in heartbroken dismay in the office that he would allow to dwindle into decline like the rest of his life.

'Mother asked me to ask you if you wouldn't mind waiting until you were back home before you opened it,' Janet urged, a look of imploring intensity burning suddenly burning in her almond shaped eyes.

'That is if I open it at all,' Alexander replied dead pan. 'That woman cannot dictate to me where, when or even if I open this envelope, regardless of what is inside. If it's a letter of apology then I don't want to read it, I am not interested in all that now, it is too late.'

'I totally understand that and there is no compunction on you to open it, but I would ask you that if you do then could you contact me straight away?' Janet says handing him a small piece of paper from her handbag containing her phone number.

' Ok. But don't wait by the phone,' Alexander said staring down at his long brown brogues.

' Well, until I hear from you again, I guess we say goodbye. Thanks just so, so much for coming today, you have no idea how much it means. Perhaps one day you will.'

And with a sincere and touching shake of Alexander's hand Janet departed. He watched as she regained the composure that had briefly eluded her and reacquainted herself with her duties. Checking around to ensure that nobody is looking, Alexander stares momentarily at his name on the front of the envelope, before neatly folding it up and placing it in the breast pocket of his suit.

' Now, where is that bloomin' brother of mine?' he whispers to himself. ' He's been in that toilet for an age...'

## 19
## REUNION

George looks at the reflection of himself in the mirror of the gents' toilets before splashing some cold water on his face and adjusting the sporadic grey hairs that crown his balding head with a faded mint green comb. A somber looking young gentleman in a pressed white shirt and skinny black tie opens the door, which George departs through with a closed lipped nod of mannerly appreciation.

He tries to look across the crowded room to see if his brother has completed his conversation with Janet, staining to straighten his bow legs on his tip toes as he does. As George's head moves from side to side, he hears a voice call faintly from behind him.

' Well George Pace. You haven't changed after all these years have you?' the female voice says in a soft lilting tone with more than a hint of a Dundee accent. In a burst of recognition, George stops dead in his tracks, straightening himself back up and dragging down his suit jacket which has ridden up higher above his waist than he would like. He inhales sharply for a moment and engages his eyes with the wooden floor in front of him before turning about, his walking stick clicking as he rotates into vision.

In front of him stands a woman, short in stature with a pleasantly pretty face which is framed by a thick head of greying curls and houses the most prominent twin set of emerald green eyes which sparkle with nervous anticipation. For a moment that lingers like a lifetime, George stands speechless, struck in awe by the vision that stands before him.

' Angela Yule, well eh'll be damned,' he finally manages to utter in a voice rasped with raw emotion. George and Angela take slow paces towards each other, each one gently closing the chasm of wasted years that have parted them. Without another word, the couple reunite in a time of grief, grasping each other in a tenderly electrifying embrace of two bodies that have been denied each other so cruelly and for so long. Tears spill out of eyes and onto shoulders which rise and fall in emotion jarring unison, clothing dampened by the express recalling of a life that might have been but has passed them by.

Angela and George split momentarily and grasp each other's cheeks tightly, staring intently into the depths of the pools of their eyes which battle between the gnawing pain of regret and unadulterated joy of reunion.

' What are you dayin here?' George manages to blurt.

' Oh George, my dear George, we have an eternal amount to catch up on. I did not expect to see you here given the circumstances. I saw you and Eck come in to the back of the church and I almost dropped my hymn book. I was sitting just about four rows in front of you. I thought it was right for me to pay my respects. Please don't think that is to condone what happened but she had contacted me in recent months whilst she was dying and I decided that I should be here,' Angela bubbled, refusing to part her clinch.

' Well, we have a lot of wasted years tae catch up on aboot each other's life. Mine's been shit, that's a yi need tae ken really!' George says half in jest to lighten the mood slightly, but entirely dripping with earnestness.

' Well without you, mine's been nothing like how it could have been. Every single day I have thought about you, how we should have been together, how we were dragged apart because of others. Deep down I knew you wouldn't get on the train that night, but I hoped so badly that you would. I knew how loyal you were to Eck and that's why I could never have blamed you. London was too far for you to be away from him but I never spent a single day that I never thought about you and what might have been,' Janet says reflectively.

' At the end of the day, the woman that's lyin' in her grave the day is the reason we split up and fir all the shit that happened. Eh never blamed you for going, you made the right move fir yirsel and there was nae danger that you could hang aroond and wait given what was goin on with me. Eh'll tell yi what, after the state he ended up in, yi must be glad yi missed oot!' George says, his face cracking into the faintest hint of mirth, as the couple allow themselves a moment of light-heartedness amongst the myriad of emotion that has engulfed them. ' You can explain all later, but briefly tell me what happened,' Angela prompts.

' Have yi got all day and night? Let's just say for noo that it totally ruined him, he lost everything. I couldn't let him lose me an all and that was why eh never boarded that train, that was the only reason. You dinna ken how much eh wanted to, but that's fir another time, if there is another time,' George says wistfully.

If there is to be another time then George will tell Angela the full undiluted truth. He will tell her how Alexander's world sunk to the bleakest depths and how the loss of his wife and then his mother prompted a lifestyle so reclusive that his business and self-esteem vanished in a haze of social phobias and self-loathing. George will tell Angela how it was he who dragged his brother out from the gutter, worked all the hours under the sun and the moon to pay Alexander's mortgage at the expense of his own council house as the bailiffs and debt collectors breathed fire down his twin's neck. He will tell her how that, despite recovering enough to face the parts of a world he hadn't previously known, Alexander's cumulative woes ultimately led them to the Riverview Nursing and Retirement home, funded by the sale of Alexander's once salubrious west end home. George will tell her how it is there that they now reside as their time cycle rolls unstoppably to its natural end, in a place where Alexander revels smugly in his pampered surroundings but where he spends every minute of every day in a world of regret and eternal dread that only she could ever have saved him from.

If there is to be another time, Angela will tell George of how she set up that small dress shop in London and there she prospered for a good while, but that her panging for her life with the man she had left in Dundee remained a persistent bitter taste in the back of her throat. She will tell George, with more than a hint of embarrassment and regret, how she had thought that she had fallen in love with a city type in London's west end with his pin striped suit and polished leather brief case a permanent accoutrement to his slicked back hair and confident, nonchalant gait. Angela will tell George that she thought that she loved him enough to tie the knot and that she did in a quiet civil ceremony in leafy suburbia. She will tell him that the discovery of the news that they couldn't have children drove a wedge between the couple, each blaming each other for their troubles. That lack of empathy, she will tell George, was the catalyst for their separation and subsequent divorce on amicable terms leading her back up the road from one capital to the other, London to Edinburgh. It was in Auld Reekie That she set up home and continues to reside in a life spent apart from that one man she knew she loved and the man she always will.

' Of course there'll be another time George,' Angela says clasping her arms around George's neck. ' We must catch up fully, but today's not the time or the place for that. And in any case, you had better get back to that brother of yours because unless he's changed outrageously since I last met him, fretting is his favourite past time!' laughs Angela, prompting the appearance of deep crows' feet aside her eyes.

' You can say that again,' George replied ruefully raising his generous eyebrows to the heavens. ' Are you sure that yi dinna want tae come oer and see him. I'm sure he'd love tae meet yi.'

' As I said George, this is not the time and the place for reunions, besides he has enough on his plate today I'm sure without me turning up to stress him out even more,' Angela says.

' Fair enough. Hopefully oor path's will cross sooner than a few decades the next time,' George jokes, his mouth cracking into a cheeky smile.

' Of Course!' Angela exclaims. ' Now give me your mobile number and I'll be in touch with you over the next few days to organise a proper catch up,' she adds, pulling her phone from out of her bag.

' A mobile, are yi joking! Eh wouldna even ken how tae work the damn thing. Listen, take this number doon and ask fir room 15 when yi get through and they'll transfer the call,' Alexander says as Angela's brow furrows.

' Oh dinna ask!' George adds ruefully, ' I will explain all next time. It doesn't even make sense to me so the day is no the day,' George says before stutteringly recalling the main number for the Riverview Nursing and Retirement Home.' Well, until next time,' the pair say, releasing each other from a vice like clinch. Angela places a soft kiss on George's wrinkled cheek sending a shiver through his body like a lightning bolt.

Without another word, she slips a piece of paper with her mobile phone number, her name and a kiss into his hand. As George watches her move through the crowd, he places the number in his wallet, next to the letter she had written him all these years ago. With every stride that he watches her take away from him he sees the years tumble backwards towards that fateful day and as she turns back to share a wave with him, George sees the image of the same Angela Jane Yule that stood on the station platform waiting forever in vain for the man she loved to sweep her aboard.

The brothers returned to the Riverview Nursing and Retirement Home that evening, Alexander having complained remorselessly that George's extended lavatory break had done little to relieve his stress, niggled with his brittle bones and most probably exacerbated his recurring problem with piles. George had elected not to inform his brother of his emotional reunion with Angela, fearing that it may distract Alexander unwantedly from his own self-pity.

The train journey home was circumspect for both brothers, the scenic greenery of Perthshire and Tayside ignored as they stared edgily out the window through kaleidoscope tinted glasses. All manner of thoughts and emotions twirled chaotically around their minds, the fusion of past and present creating an uncertain future coloured by a heady mix of darkness and light, a twisty frenzy of emotions yet to be unopened.

Alexander had briefly, at the start of the journey, confided in George about his doubts over whether to open the envelope that remained unopened in the breast pocket of his suit. Today was supposed to represent the ultimate closure for Alexander, the locking of the door on years of trouble and strife inflicted by the snide actions of his trouble and strife. If he opens the envelope, he mused, will the contents reopen a can infested with worms that he had hoped he could glue closed today? Alternatively, would the letter's contents place an indelible full stop on a murky chapter that has determined the entire course of his life? The agony of choice.

' I will sleep on it George,' he says to his brother as they lie in their beds in the moodily decorated twin room, which lies cloaked in darkness save an amber glow from the street lamp outside. ' What with the migraine I have from today's stress and my dangerously high blood pressure, it would be silly to make rash decisions tonight.'

George doesn't ignore him, he just doesn't really hear him. He is lost in the memories of his meeting with his former sweetheart Angela and, like a lovesick schoolboy, pangs for the day that he speaks to her again. Will he call her first or will that seem desperate? God knows, she even might be married, he thinks to himself, though he spotted that she was not wearing a wedding ring. Does that mean anything? Is it a sign?

' You know I had this totally vivid dream last night George,' Alexander says sitting up on his pillow.

' You're no aboot tae tell me what the dream is are yi? Honestly, that's one oh meh pet hates, people boring me tae death we their dreams. It's boring enough people bleatin' on aboot what did happen tae them never mind takin up yir time tellin yi aboot somethin' that didnae,' George grunted, turning aggressively to face the wall.

Alexander ignores him, ' Well, the dream was so detailed that it felt like it actually has happened to me. In the dream I was leaving Asda, you know the one in Kirkton, with a trolley full of groceries and, looking to my left, there was a kiosk with steel shutter type doors. There was a lady standing inside the kiosk with four men who were wearing white masks, you know like the forensic police would wear? Anyway, I asked the lady what was going on because, you know me George, I am generally a nosey person. She started telling me 'blah, blah, blah, blah.' But here's the strange part- leaving the shop she followed me out and was reading out her phone number and I asked her for a pencil to write it down on a piece of paper, which she gave me. I asked the woman her name and she replied but I couldn't make out what she was saying, even when she repeated it over and over again. Then she was gone and I was left standing with a piece of paper with her number on it. When I woke up this morning, I could remember the number as clear as day, like I had been dialing it all my life. I am contemplating dialing it tomorrow, but that would probably confirm that I am mad! Anyway, the number was so clear that it was freaky so I wrote it down this morning here on the paper beside my bed lamp. Eh George, are you sleeping?' Alexander asks, squinting his eyes across the room.

George lies wide awake. He is staring at the wall in front of him contemplating whether he should throw his slipper at his brother's mouth or just wait long enough for him to run out of steam, which he knows he always does.

20

A LONG HUG

The brothers awake to their radio alarm, which blinks alive at 7.02 am, the sound of a cheery sounding Tay FM newsreader stirring the collective consciousness of the brothers who have both endured interminably sleepless nights. When Alexander had said he was going to sleep on it, the assumption was that he was going to sleep. That inference should not necessarily have been taken for granted. Sleep was something he had just done little enough of.

But he had made his last and final decision about the envelope, 'I am going to destroy it George,' he says to his twin brother with finality.

' The envelope?' George asks rhetorically, dragging his creaking limbs out of his creaking bed and onto his creaking feet.

' Yes, the envelope George, what else would I be talking about?' Alexander tuts, with an incredulity that blurs into rudeness.

' Eh, well eh thought yi meant my life when you said you were going to destroy it. Oh, sorry, you've already done that eh?' George replies with an acidic mirth cloaking a deep seated gripe.

' No, *she* ruined our lives and that is the reason why I'm destroying the envelope. Yesterday's funeral was seminal for me. She's dead now, out of my life, there's nothing in this envelope that can make up for what we had to go through George,' Alexander uses the royal 'we' as he stares at the white envelope that has lurked over him all night from its viewpoint on his bedside cabinet, perched neatly between his copy of Shakespeare's sonnet 60 and his photograph of his mother.

Alexander sneers diffidently in the envelope's direction.

' Well as long as yir sure Eck, you dae that,' George says limping gingery across the room towards his walking stick which is leaning absentmindedly against his brother's bedside cabinet, just below the envelope.

Picking up the stick, George glances at the envelope briefly before his eye is averted by a smaller piece of torn white paper on the cabinet.

' What is this?' George asks, a hint of panicked tremor faintly audible in his voice.

' It's that number, you know the phone number from the dream I was telling you about last night? You know when you were pretending to be asleep but were really listening?' Alexander replies nonchalantly.

' Eh wis asleep. You would be asleep too if yi had tae listen tae you bleating on all the time. Yir like a talking sleepin pill,' George agitates, pretending to be clueless despite his full knowledge of the dream. He looks at the number again, checks it twice, three, four times through. There is something familiar about it.

He rushes as fast as his walking stick will carry him over to his wallet, which sits on his own bedside locker. Opening it, he claws for Angela's number within. To his utter astonishment it is the identical number that Alexander had written down from the promptings of the woman in his dream.

' Where did yi get this number?' George asks, half perplexed, half panicked.

' I told you last night, if you'd cared to have listened properly then you would know. It's from a dream I had, the number was so vivid I had to write it down,' Alexander retorts looking up at George above the fingernails he is pretending to check for dirt.

' This cannae be right, are you takin the piss oot oh me noo are yi?' George agitates. 'Listen, eh wis listenin tae yir dream all alang, but eh need yi tae tell me fir real, where the hell did ye get this number fae?' George's voice is rising considerably in octaves.

' What on earth is the matter George?' Alexander asks sitting upright on the puffed up pillows of his bed. ' What do you mean about the number? It's the one from my dream. George, you look as though you've seen a ghost, ' Alexander says as he shuffles to a position of comfort and control.

Ashen faced, George proceeds to blurt out everything about his meeting with Angela outside the bathroom at Mary's funeral. He tells his brother, in his own brusque terms, of that heart stopping moment when she called his name and he turned to see the vision that he was certain had been consigned to the faint reaches of the past. George described the tears and the emotions, the heart rending clinch he had waited so long for and never considered would happen in reality. He explains, in a condition of rare outward emotion, that he was unsure of whether to contact Angela again or let bygones be bygones and move on with the life he had assumed without her. A life he endures rather than enjoys.

' So, what has that got to do with the phone number from my dream?' Alexander agitated, his mind whirring like a dervish about the possibilities that a brief reunion may have opened up for his brother, and more saliently, himself.

' Because, Eck, Angela gave me her phone number and told me tae give her a call, it was her mobile number. Now the number she gave me is the exact same number as the one you wrote doon fae yir dream. Look at the twa o them. How is that even possible?' George shrieks, thrusting the two numbers in front of Alexander who squints as they blur into his vision.

Alexander checks the numbers like a man who thinks he may have drawn the six winning numbers from the lottery, his eyes darting from one torn shred of paper to the next.

' That is remarkable George, truly remarkable, truly unbe-bloodylievable' Alexander says shaking his head disbelievingly. ' I knew there was something spooky about that dream, I knew it. Everything in it was just so clear in my head, particularly the phone number. You know what this is George?' Alexander asks.

' What is it?'

' Fate. You are meant to call her. This is a message from above, it is what is meant to be. It also shows the powers we possess as twins, to know how each other is feeling, what each other is thinking. Call her George, call her today,' Alexander implores, his voice quivering slightly with a tinge of underlying reluctance.

George sits on his bed and leans contemplatively for a few moments, filling the air with the uncertain noise of quietness. Rubbing the hairs at the side of his head he inhales short, sharp pockets of air.

' If eh do call her Eck, it disnae mean eh'll be leavin you.' George says engaging his twin brother's eyes as he breaks the brevity of nothingness. 'Eh dinnae even ken whit she is doin these days, she might be married we bairns and grandbairns fir all eh ken. But, believe me Eck, no matter what, eh would never, ever leave you in the lurch. No matter what.' George emotes strongly as he walks across the room before placing his hand on his brother's shoulder.

Alexander pats his brothers hand three times in gentle tenderness. ' Listen, you do what you have to do. Do not worry about me. If yesterday told me anything it is that I have wasted too much of my life worrying about that woman and, in doing so, I have wasted yours too. That is something I truly regret and those are years and times that you can never buy back,' Alexander's voice is dripping with a sincerity rarely heard in his voice

He continues, 'I am happy with my lot now, living here and seeing my time through, but you have more to offer than me. My life's been and gone, it left me many years ago never to return. That's why I'm destroying the envelope, the past is the past and we need to move on with our lives,' Alexander's impassioned words are tinged with a

149

steely intent and diluted by welling tears.

' Today's the start of the rest of our lives George. Whatever those lives bring we cannot be dictated by events of the past any longer.' And with that the brothers stare into each other' eyes and try to ignore each other's tears. Then they do something so rare that it feels almost seminal- they share a hug.

# 21
## FUTURE

Alexander sits at the bandstand on Magdalen Green, the mid-summer sun warming the early morning air and painting an orange glow on the waters beneath the steel gilders of the Tay Rail Bridge. He looks out at the river and watches the waves ripple gently against the wall at Dundee's Riverside. He thinks of Shakespeare's sonnet number 60 and how each wave lapping against the shore represents a memory that comes and goes, never to be returned, no second to ever be recaptured. But there is a calmness to the water today; gentle ripples almost holding time still, the destructive waves lying dormant in distant seas waiting for another day to cajole them.

He thinks of Gatsby from the novel he adored at school. Gatsby was a man without a history, whose eyes were always searching for something, someone that he never had. Gatsby believed in the green light and of the future. For Alexander, the amber glow that the sun has encouraged onto the peacefully calm river glares into Alexander's eyes like the shining crossroads of his life. Alexander holds the envelope in his left hand, it is history, his someone, his something and he is ready to consign it with the relics of the past. Only once it is turned to the flames of amber will the green light of the future shine bright in his mind.

Taking a lighter from his trouser pocket, he hangs the envelope up to the amber sun with his trembling left hand and sparks the light with his right. Holding the flame under the paper, a tsunami of memories and voices rush around his mind. Just as he moves the flame closer a slender shadow suddenly skulks over him, painting a long dark picture across his bows. With a jolt he stops, the amber light turns to darkness.

' Don't do it Dad, please, don't!' a voice calls pleadingly from behind. A moment freezes over, the waves of time momentarily stop, a ripple recedes to the stillness of nothing- no sound, no movement, just the blankness of nothing.

The voice is somehow familiar to Alexander, but the words aren't. It is a voice he recognizes, not from the past, but the present. As if in slow motion he turns in his chair, standing slowly as he sees a female with pale, porcelain skin dressed smartly in blue skinny jeans and nude court shoes, a chiffon cardigan tied around her slender shoulders. Alexander squints and fixes his large, almond shaped, deep brown eyes on her large, almond shaped, deep brown eyes. He clicks off the lighter and allows the envelope to fall to the floor of the bandstand.

' Janet, is that you? What did you just call me?' he asks, seeking confirmation that the words were not merely a blurred figment of his imagination.

' I said don't do it dad, don't burn the letter. And yes, you are my dad,' Janet says with a firm croak of emotion, inching cautiously towards Alexander.

Shifting backwards, Alexander stutters, ' Wh.., wh…., what on earth are you talking about, wh…., wh….. why are you saying this to me?'

' Look in the envelope, it is what mother is wanting to tell you. I know this is extremely difficult for you to hear, it was for me too, but I am telling you the God's honest truth. You are my dad,' Janet says in a tone that offers little room for doubt.

Suddenly Alexander erupts, ' What are you talking about, how is this possible? Why are you coming here now trying to ruin my life with these lies?! Be off with you now, I have never heard such preposterous nonsense in all my life. Your father is dead, just like your mother and good riddance to them both, now get out of my way,' he screams, rising to his feet to escape the impassioned utterings of the woman who claims to be his offspring, a love child spawned out of one way love.

' But look at me dad, look at my eyes, they are the same as yours, my height, my build, everything about me, it is undeniable. I know this is a total shock, but you really are my dad. You are me. You made me,' Janet implores grabbing the cuff of Alexander's shirt to prevent him departing her presence.

Staring, directly and straight into Janet's eyes, Alexander's mind suddenly works in a whirling flux of rewind, spinning back to query the possibilities of Janet's seemingly preposterous claims. But she is correct in many things she has said; most significantly she is almost as familiar to him as the image he sees in the mirror every morning. Working back to what could now be the future, he recollects his last night of 'passion' with Janet's mother, a woman's whose name he hates to utter and whose memory he wished to finally incinerate in the past with the flick of a lighter.

The words from a letter long since delivered in spite are imprinted like indelible ink on his brain, a final insult so hurting that it has tattooed infinitely  his mind: 'When we made love last week I felt nothing, no passion or desire and it was then that I knew our time was over. I tried to win back that spark but it was gone.'

The words stab like a knife as he reads them in his mind, but here in front of him stands a beautiful woman who is claiming to be the embodiment of that so-called union, the manifestation of one way love.

' How old are you and when is your birthday?' a flustering Alexander demands.

' I'm 34, I'll be 35 in August,' Janet replies with assuredness.

Alexander's brain whirrs through arithmetic calculations. Janet's suggestion fits with the dates in his mind. The suggestion that he has fathered this woman is suddenly waning somewhat in its preposterousness. Alexander shakes his head like a flee ridden dog, clutching at his temples with his trembling skeletal hands.

' I feel faint,' he says sitting down on the bench that overlooks the River Tay. Janet sits beside him and places a soft, comforting hand on his knee.

' This is tough for me too but it is true, you are my dad. I am so sorry that it has come to this, but I can only tell you what is the truth.' They share a lingering look, partly of disbelief, partly of realisation, partly of wonder, wholly of regret.

' How is this true? When did you know about this?' Alexander asks as he begins to come to some kind of terms with reality.

' When my father was ill he needed blood transfusions to prolong his life, the cancer had made him terribly weak. The hospital was running short on blood of his blood type so I went in to give some of my own. After I left the hospital one of the doctors called mother in and said that they couldn't use my blood to help my father because our blood types were different, which the doctor said was rare but not unique. It didn't necessarily mean that I wasn't father's daughter, but it was the final piece of the jigsaw as far as mum was concerned- she eventually said that she had suspected for a long number of years that you might be my dad and that my father wasn't, but she had kept her suspicions to herself and hoped that it would never be discovered,' Janet started, her fingers gently stroking Alexander's hand as she speaks in soothing tones.

' So there again is yet more deceit from your mother if you, or indeed she, is to be believed,' Alexander snaps suddenly like an dog who has been prodded with a hot poker. ' What made her suspect that you were mine and did your father learn of this?' he probes as he recovers a degree of composure.

' Mainly by the way I looked, she thought I was the image of you from a young age, she even said she would style my hair in a way that made my resemblance to you somehow remain unnoticed by others- even dad. The date of my birth and her calendar calculations always made it a possibility in her, but she tried to deny herself from thinking it. Mum said that she simply convinced herself that father was the real dad and by doing that she tried to ignore the feelings of guilt and remorse that would envelope her sometimes, but, to her, ignorance was relative bliss. When the doctors said that the bloods didn't match then she wasn't shocked, but she would have preferred not to have had this further piece of evidence.

' Dad never knew, mum never told him, he was very poorly when it was ultimately confirmed in her head and she didn't see the need to distress him further. I don't know if he was suspicious, especially given the date of my birth and my resemblance to you, but if he was he certainly never let on. He was a great father to me, that's all I can say and this doesn't change anything in that respect. But you are my dad,' Janet says, her voice bubbling and cracking with emotion.

Alexander inhales, inhales and inhales until he has sharply sucked the oxygen out of the air and into his befuddled mind which contains a myriad of thoughts and feelings that battle with each other to make sense. What Janet has just told Alexander ties together logically in his head and is eminently plausible. However, in reality, if she is speaking in facts it is a revelation far too grand for him to comprehend.

Consumed by a mind full of befuddling possibilities, Alexander holds the white envelope up to a sky cloaked in a wispy mixture of grey and white clouds as miniscule, insignificant freckles of precipitation faintly tickle the roof of the bandstand above their heads. Flicking on his lighter, he also pulls a faded, yellowed piece of paper from inside his shirt pocket and holds both letters beneath the amber flame. Janet moves to stop him, but Alexander denies her the chance, holding his long index finger to her rouged lips and warning her down from her feet.

As he sets the corner of the envelope alight, he drops it onto the ground as the flame quickly gnarls and swallows the paper which turns to orange gold in front of their almond shaped eyes. Father and daughter watch silently as the smoking embers of his past limbo dance skywards to darken the wispy clouds.

' Why did you do that dad?' Janet asks staring down at the ashes a letters from the past and the secret contents of an envelope never to be unearthed or uncovered.

Alexander pauses for what seems like a lifetime, contemplating his thoughts and impulses. ' Because what was in that envelope was irrelevant to me,' he finally blurts, engaging eye contact with Janet. ' I will never know, nor do I need to know what was in that letter. Your mother left me by a letter and I have now delivered her that one back, along with this one you delivered to me on her behalf. Her words mean nothing to me now. She wrote the words 35 years ago that have haunted me ever since and now those words have joined her- to you in heaven, to me in Hell. You have told me everything I need to know Janet. You the beautiful daughter I always craved but never knew existed. I believe that fully now,' Alexander sobs, his watery eyes tracking the smoking embers skywards.

Finally united out of the tangled web of lost years, Alexander and Janet wail tears of grief, regret, despair and underlying happiness. A past of deceit and lies has unraveled to this moment. Clinging on to his daughter, Alexander's chin rests on her shoulder, his welled eyes staring out into the distance. There, in his mind, he pictures a vision of the waves as they slowly recede back from the shore, each one

156

representing a year lost that he can never recapture. With each receding wave he imagines an image of his daughter growing up year by year- from her first vision of light to the first step taken, from the first day a school to graduation, from the troubles of adolescence to her honeymoon vacation. These are photographs in his mind that he had never before imagined and, as the waves wash the images clear, he sees a picture of himself clearly. He sees himself in the future, recapturing time, unburdened by bitterness, freed from the burden of anger. It is the image he saw when he looked in the mirror before his life was turned upside down forever.

' Well, I guess that we have a lot of years to catch up on Janet,' he manages to blurt out as he holds her porcelain cheeks in his wrinkled palms. ' A new future starts today and I hope that you'll have me in yours.'

Janet nods an emotion drenched affirmation and claps her dad's hands in hers. Unnoticed to them both, the re-emerging sunlight has invited the formation of the shadow of a couple who stand watching from the pavement of the street above Magdalen Green.

There George Pace and Angela Yule stand looking down with arms linked, sharing a moment of dawning realization. Offering each other a knowing nod, Angela pulls a handkerchief from her purse and passes it to George. He uses it to dab his eye and, for a moment, he allows his mind to spin to the future before he returns to the realities of the present. With that the couple wordlessly turn and slowly walk towards the next chapter of all of their lives.

## 22
## FATE

Three weeks later:

Twin brothers George and Alexander Pace sit side by side under the bandstand at Magdalen Green, a faint wind whistling a wistful lullaby under their noses. Dressed smartly in pressed trousers, polished shoes and collared shirts each with an old, brown leather suitcase at their feet. In the distance behind them, the Riverview Nursing and Retirement Home loiters, a lingering reminder of what had appeared to be the brothers' steady decline towards their inevitable fate.

' Well George, today is the beginning of our new lives, the first step towards a better future,' Alexander says interrupting the peaceful setting.

' Eh, it's a pity it's aboot 40 years too late but never mind Eck! The best things come to those who wait eh?' George retorts with a typically sarcastic mirth.

' Yes, well, very funny. Anyway, we said we'd move on from the past now George. I must say I'll miss the old place though, won't you?' Alexander replies nodding his head vaguely in direction of the Riverview Nursing and Retirement Home. George doesn't even afford it a glance.

' Eh, eh'll miss it like a hole in the heid! You're just worried that yi'll no have bloody Nurse Mable rubbin creams on yir back. Wha's gonna plump up yir pillows and make yir breakfast in that new hoose that yir renting cos yi needn't imagine that eh'll be comin roond tae dae all yir dirty work fir yi!' George chuckles ruefully.

'I can look after myself just perfectly thank you George, even with the rheumatism and the brittle bones and the constant threat of a migraine. Anyhow, Janet says she will be coming down a day a week and that I'll be going to see her and my grandchild in Perth once a week so I won't be too lonely thank you,' Alexander replies puffing out his chest.

' At least I won't have to listen to you moaning and groaning every minute of the day, I hope that Angela knows what she is letting herself in for!' Alexander says, nudging his brother with his sharp elbow.

' Well, as eh said, she's saying that we're takin it easy eh? We are just friends again but we'll see how it goes. She's gonna come down a couple of weekends a month, we've many years tae catch up on and a lot o water has run under the bridge but we'll see how it all goes. So nae doubt we'll hae enough time on oor hands fir you tae pester me. Jist dinnae drag me tae any mare funerals Eck, unless it's meh ain,' George urges jocularly.

' Don't worry George I won't. Anyway, I'm sure I'll be first to go, what with my brittle…'

' Bones and migraines and rheumatism and anxiety attacks and all the rest!' George interrupts aping his brother's accent with a snooty voice. ' Save it for Janet tae listen tae, you might get some sympathy there!' The two brothers laugh heartily before George asks, 'Jist tell me one thing before oor taxi arrives.'

' What's that George?'

' Did you really dream Angela's phone number that night or had you seen me at the funeral speakin' tae her and gone huntin' in meh wallet?' George inquires pensively.

Alexander contemplates for a few seconds then says, ' Let's just call it fate…...'

He winks at George before standing and helping his brother to his feet with the offering of his hand. The brothers put their arms around each other's shoulders briefly and exchange a pursed lipped nod. Alexander picks up a suitcase in each hand and allows George to limp unburdened with his walking stick.

 Leaving the bandstand the twins cut contrasting figures as they walk towards a taxi which toots as it waits before turning off its amber light to green as the driver emerges to help the brothers with their luggage. Momentarily Alexander turns and has a lingering glance out at the moody River Tay where the sun shimmers laconically on the still silver water, the peaceful scene punctuated only by the cawing of a storm crow and the faint sigh of a commuter train wheezing intently over the imposing steel girders of the rail bridge which sweeps majestically across to the lazy shores of Fife.

He watches as a solitary wave laps against the river wall, slowly corroding, one by one, the destructive memories of the past. As the wave retreats and reverses it seems to reclaim lost time. For Alexander, his sequent toil is over, his waters calmed in hope that life's hand may, at last, deal him and his brother a better fate.

 A fate better than life……..

## ACKNOWLEDGEMENTS

With grateful thanks to everyone who took an interest in the production of this book. A big thank you to Mary O'Brien for her help and to Kirk and Victoria Dailly for working on design. My gratitude further extends to Christian and Kirk Dailly for their initial reading and advice. Finally to my wife and family for listening to me drone on about 'my book'!

3326082R00099

Printed in Germany
by Amazon Distribution
GmbH, Leipzig